SHERLOCK HOLMES

The Grand Horizontals

***also published by Black Coat Press
in the same series***

Arsène Lupin vs. Sherlock Holmes: The Hollow Needle
(*adapted from Maurice Leblanc
by Jean-Marc & Randy Lofficier*)

Arsène Lupin vs. Sherlock Holmes: The Blonde Phantom
(*adapted from Maurice Leblanc
by Jean-Marc & Randy Lofficier*)

Arsène Lupin vs. Sherlock Holmes: The Stage Play
(*adapted from Victor Darlay & Henry de Gorsse
by Frank J. Morlock*)

also by Frank J. Morlock

Lord Ruthven the Vampire
(*John William Polidori &
adapted from Charles Nodier and Eugène Scribe*)

The Return of Lord Ruthven
(*adapted from Alexandre Dumas*)

Frankenstein Meets the Hunchback of Notre-Dame
(*adapted from Charles Nodier, Antoine Nicolas Béraud &
Jean Toussaint Merle and Victor Hugo, Paul Foucher
& Paul Meurice*)

Sherlock Holmes

The Grand Horizontals

by
Frank J. Morlock

A Black Coat Press Book

Acknowledgements: We are indebted to Dagny for typing the plays and David McDonnell for proofreading the typescript.

This book is dedicated to Alan Segal, my friend and doctor.

Sherlock Holmes created by Sir Arthur Conan Doyle.
Fantômas created by Marcel Allain & Pierre Souvestre.
Father Brown created by G. K. Chesterton.

The Grand Horizontals Copyright © 1982, 2005 by Frank J. Morlock.
The Adventure of Merlin's Tomb, *The Adventure of the Mulberry Street Irregular* Copyright © 1985 by Frank J. Morlock.
The Man Who Fell From Heaven Copyright © 2002 by Frank J. Morlock.
The Curious Circumstance of the Maid's Mustache Copyright © 2003 by Frank J. Morlock.
Clash of the Vampires, *The Silent Treatment* © 2005 by Frank J. Morlock.

Cover illustration Copyright © 1999 by Philippe Jozelon.

Visit our website at www.blackcoatpress.com

ISBN 1-932983-47-3. First Printing. January 2006. Published by Black Coat Press, an imprint of Hollywood Comics.com, LLC, P.O. Box 17270, Encino, CA 91416. All rights reserved. Except for review purposes, no part of this book may be reproduced or transmitted in any form or by any means, electronic or mechanical, including photocopying, recording or by any information storage and retrieval system, without permission in writing from the publisher. The stories and characters depicted in this book are entirely fictional. Printed in the United States of America.

Table of Contents

The Grand Horizontals 7
    Act I 11
    Act II 34
    Act III 51
    Epilogue 67
The Adventure of Merlin's Tomb 69
The Adventure of the Mulberry Street Irregular 103
The Man Who Fell From Heaven 143
Clash of the Vampires 183
The Silent Treatment 203
The Curious Circumstance of the Maid's Mustache ... 219

The Grand Horizontals

(*Sherlock Holmes and Fantômas*)

Characters

Sherlock Holmes, a consulting detective
Dr. Watson, his roommate and confidant
Caroline Otero, a Grand Horizontal
Liane de Pougy, another Grand Horizontal
Le Biffon, Liane's bodyguard
The Grand Duke of Graustark
Baron Ollstreder
Fantômas
Mrs. Hudson
Two bouncers
Servants

Act I

Scene I
221B Baker Street

A beautiful day in April. The time: mid-afternoon. Holmes is seated on the ottoman smoking his pipe, reading some papers. Watson, who is more affected by the weather than Holmes, is getting restless.

WATSON: What a glorious day, Holmes!
HOLMES (*perusing his papers*): Umm!
WATSON: What's wrong, Holmes?
HOLMES: *That man* is up to something again. (*He sinks back into his thoughts.*)
WATSON: What man, Holmes?
HOLMES: Fantômas.
WATSON: Ah, yes. I read about him recently. He was just in London, wasn't he? The papers referred to him by some kind of funny sobriquet...
HOLMES: The "Lord of Terror."
WATSON: The "Lord of Terror." Fancy that.
HOLMES: Yes, Watson, the French are strangely proud of their monsters–but this time, I think I know what they're up to...

(*With that, Holmes relapses into silence, puffs on his pipe and begins to study some notes, uttering a series of small grunts and exclamations, half under his breath.*)

HOLMES (*barely audible*): Clever that–very clever that. But how shall I prove it?

(*He slowly sinks back into lethargy. But Watson has lost interest and feels the call of Spring.*)

WATSON: I don't for the life of me see how you can just sit there so indifferently when nature is blessing us with such beautiful weather. It's Spring.

(*Watson gets up and paces about.*)

HOLMES: I envy your enthusiasm, Watson.
WATSON (*going to the bay window*): It's glorious, simply glorious. (*looking out*) I say. That's odd. Come here, Holmes.

(*Holmes rises and goes to the window.*)

HOLMES: What is it?
WATSON: That woman, she can't be coming here.
HOLMES (*looking*): I believe she is, Watson.
WATSON: Good Heavens, Holmes! She–she looks like a French whore!
HOLMES: That is the single most observant remark I have ever heard you make, Watson. I have hopes for you yet, dear fellow.
WATSON (*stuffily*): I'm glad Mrs. Hudson is not home. Whatever would she think?
HOLMES: I'm sure her views on the subject would be most interesting–though frankly, Watson, I'm glad I shall not have to hear them.
WATSON: She's here, I think.

(*Enter Caroline Otero, without a knock. She is drop dead gorgeous, somewhere in her twenties; her assurance is unspeakable; her charm thoroughly disconcerting; her effect on men–overwhelming. She is dressed in an outrageous decolleté ensemble, complete with parasol and decorated hat.*)

CAROLINE (*with a French accent*): Allo! I'm come to see M'sieur Sherlock Holmès.
HOLMES (*bowing stiffly*): I am at your service, Madame.
CAROLINE: You may call me Caroline. I'm known as *La Belle Otero*–but if I like you, you may call me Caroline. And (*grandly*) I *do* like you. Yes, I'm sure we shall be great friends.
HOLMES (*with a touch of irony*): I am flattered.
CAROLINE: I hope I'm not disturb you, M'sieur Holmès?
HOLMES (*ironic and gallant*): Actually, I find your presence quite disturbing.
CAROLINE: Oh, you are such a *gentilhomme*, M'sieur Holmès. Now, me, I am flattered.
HOLMES: This is my colleague, Doctor Watson.
WATSON (*bows and preens a little*): Enchanté, Mademoiselle.
CAROLINE: Ah, Monsieur is *le Docteur*? They never told me you are so handsome.
WATSON (*delighted*): Mademoiselle is too kind.

(*Caroline now sets herself in motion, inspecting the room with the curiosity of a month-old kitten. She flits about, picking things up, pointing to them with her parasol, delighted as a child with a caravan of new toys.*)

CAROLINE (*pointing at a microscope*): *Qu'est-ce que c'est que ça?*
HOLMES: That is my microscope.
CAROLINE (*pointing at something else*): *Ah, très intéressant. Et ça?*
HOLMES (*nettled*): Are you touring London, Mademoiselle, or have you some business with me?
CAROLINE: Oh, *pardonnez-moi*, M'sieur Holmès. I'm so–*distraite*–I think everything 'ere is so impressive that I almost forget why I come.
HOLMES: Yes. Why did you come?
CAROLINE: To see you, of course–the greatest detective–
HOLMES: It might be helpful if you would explain.
CAROLINE: Somebody is killing my gentlemen friend. Is not nice. I want you please to stop them.
HOLMES: Someone has killed your "gentlemen friend?"
CAROLINE: Yes. And not just one.
HOLMES: You have more than one?
CAROLINE: Oh, I have many. It is–how to say it?–bad for business when they die. Two dead already–three very soon. Terrible.
HOLMES: Let's start at the beginning. Tell us something about yourself. You can speak before Doctor Watson. You must not be shy–
CAROLINE: Shy? I'm never shy! I'm Caroline Otero! I'm born in Spain. Three years ago, I come to Paris as an *artiste*, a *danseuse*. (*She executes a flawless and seductive ballet movement.*) The best in Paris–all of France. The whole world loves to see me dance. Nobody dances like me. (*executing a bump and grind.*) Many gentlemen fall in love with me. They can't help. I fall in

love with them. I can't help, too. They're all so nice to me. One man in particular–he's very nice. He give me flowers, jewels, furs–even a big house in Passy. His name is–was–Georges de Champmas. We were very happy together, Georges and I, for more than a year. Nobody was ever happier. But one day, big fight. All over. Finished.

HOLMES: Was there any reason for the quarrel?

CAROLINE: None at all. Georges, he is crazy, jealous. *Complètement fou*. He dare to accuse me of having other lovers.

WATSON: The cad!

CAROLINE (*pouting*): *C'est vrai*. So we part. I keep everything, the house, all my jewels. Now, I'm alone. What a girl to do? So I meet Henri. Henri Havard. Was a banker.

HOLMES: I believe he is well-known, even in London.

CAROLINE: Henri is–was–so kind. A little old, a little fat, but never mean–and never jealous, ever. Oh, how I try to make that man jealous. But that old man was too smart to get jealous of a young woman like me. Now, that man, he knew how to treat a woman.

HOLMES: To be sure. But what happened?

CAROLINE: Then I meet Philippe. Philippe Denizou. He is rich, even more than Henri. He is merely a bourgeois–but so handsome and so generous...

HOLMES: This is very interesting, Mademoiselle Otero, but who exactly got killed?

CAROLINE: *Ah oui*. About two months ago, Georges is strangled with a woman's stocking.

WATSON: Good Heaven, how horrible.

CAROLINE: *Oui*. I thought it amusing at first. You see, I never thought Georges like that sort of thing.

Strangulation, I mean. But he did have a fetish about silk stockings. Always, I have to wear silk stockings when–
HOLMES: I see, I see. Go on.
WATSON (*excited*): You always wear–(*hushed*) what color...?
HOLMES: Not now, Watson.
CAROLINE: Anyway, who care about Georges, I say? Then, two weeks later, Henri, he, too, is strangled.
WATSON (*hotly*): With a woman's stocking?
CAROLINE: *Oui!* Now, I feel sorry for poor Henri. He was so nice to me. But first, I think it is connected with his business at the bank, not me. Except that the Police, they find a note which says: "*He who loves Caroline dies.*"
WATSON: This is nothing short of amazing.
CAROLINE: It's very sad, very sad. To love me is to die! (*She nevertheless says this with a certain air of satisfaction.*)
WATSON: Oh, don't think like that; oh you poor girl–
CAROLINE: Why not? If it's true. I am the *femme fatale*.
HOLMES: And what has happened to Philippe?
CAROLINE: Ah, that's more sad than the others. He run away and hide, the coward.
HOLMES: So Philippe Denizou is then still alive?
CAROLINE: *Oui*–if they don't get him soon. But he was alive when I left Paris.
HOLMES: Hmm! Is there some unrequited lover, who perhaps–?
CAROLINE: Unrequited lover? Ah, ah, ah! No, M'sieur Holmès. All men who love me, they have been requited.
HOLMES: I see. Then you have no suspicions?
CAROLINE: Suspicions. Of course, I have suspicions. *Certainement!* I know who did it, very exactly.

HOLMES: Who?
CAROLINE: Liane de Pougy!
WATSON: A woman!
CAROLINE: *Bien sur!* Who but a woman would do such a thing? A thing so spiteful.
HOLMES: But why?
CAROLINE: To make me so feared I can't have anymore gentlemen friends.
WATSON: Er, why would she want to do that?
CAROLINE: Because I have more and better friends than she has.
HOLMES: I shall try to put this delicately. You mean, from professional rivalry?
CAROLINE: *Absolument!*
WATSON: Holmes, in all my years of working with you, I never heard of such a thing.
HOLMES: Nor I, Watson. But it's not beyond the realm of possibility.
WATSON: But how could a woman, a member of the fair sex, the weaker sex, strangle a man?
CAROLINE: For a woman like me, it would be very easy. I'm very strong.
HOLMES: Ah! And this Liane de Pougy, is she exceptionally strong?
CAROLINE (*scornfully*): *Oh, non!* She is small and *petite* like a starved chicken. Flat too. (*gesture of contempt.*)
WATSON: Then, it seems your suspicions are groundless?
CAROLINE: *Pas du tout.* She has a big boy friend–a bodyguard, he used to be a wrestler. Big like an elephant.
HOLMES: And his name?
CAROLINE: Le Biffon.

HOLMES: I assume Liane de Pougy and her henchman, Le Biffon, are now in Paris?
CAROLINE: *Non*. They follow me here. They are in London. (*looking out the window*) I think that is him over there, leaning against the lampost across the street.

(*Holmes rushes towards the door with lightning speed.*)

HOLMES: Quickly, Watson! Will you stay here, Mademoiselle? We will return in a moment.

(*Holmes and Watson exit while Caroline amuses herself by poking her parasol at various things. Soon, they return with Le Biffon, a gigantic but apparently simple-minded man in tow.*)

HOLMES (*entering*): Come! Doctor Watson is an excellent shot and will not hesitate to demonstrate his skill as a marksman if you resist.
CAROLINE: Ah, you have captured the big ape. (*to Le Biffon*) Why did you kill my friends?
LE BIFFON: I never kill your friends. I never kill anybody.
CAROLINE: What you follow me for, then?
LE BIFFON: Liane told me to.
CAROLINE: *La garce!*
HOLMES (*to Le Biffon*): You are suspected of murdering two men at the request of your mistress, Liane de Pougy. Do you deny it?
LE BIFFON: Of course, I deny it. Do you take me for a fool? I would be a fool to not deny it, even if I did it!
HOLMES: That is not an answer calculated to convince one of your honesty.

LE BIFFON: I don't try to convince you of anything. You asked a question, I gave an answer.
CAROLINE: What a thug, eh, M'sieur Holmès? He looks just like a murderer, too. Brute!
HOLMES (*to Le Biffon*): I have more questions to put to you.
LE BIFFON: Eh, I have no more answers.
WATSON: What shall we do, Holmes? Shall I get the Police?
LE BIFFON: Get the Police. I am not wanted for any offense.
HOLMES: I am afraid we shall have to let him go, Watson.
CAROLINE: Let me try, M'sieur Holmès.
HOLMES: If you like.
CAROLINE (*preening in front of Le Biffon who is visibly aroused*): Liane is pretty, Le Biffon, but do you not think I am pretty, too?
LE BIFFON: *Oui.*
CAROLINE: I have always liked you, Le Biffon, even if your taste in women so far has proven execrable.
LE BIFFON: Mademoiselle is too kind–
CAROLINE: Just because a big man like you likes a scrawny chicken does not mean he has nothing good in him. (*She moves closer to him*) I think there is good in you, no, Le Biffon?
LE BIFFON (*his eyes are bulging*): Ah, er, Mademoiselle–
CAROLINE: If you tell me everything, Le Biffon, I will let you untie my boots.
LE BIFFON (*breathing stentoriously*): Oh, Mademoiselle!
CAROLINE: And if you tell the whole truth and nothing but, you know what I'll do for you, Le Biffon?

LE BIFFON (*almost in a paroxysm*): No, Mademoiselle–
CAROLINE: If you tell the whole truth, after you untie my shoe, I'll whip you with my riding crop.
LE BIFFON (*convulsively*): AAHH!
CAROLINE: So you will tell, *non?*
LE BIFFON: I will, I will!
CAROLINE: Anyone who knows me knows I always keep my word. Speak!
LE BIFFON (*weeping*): Unfortunately, I know nothing. I could kill myself.
CAROLINE (*totally disgusted*): *Ah l'animal!* Go–get away from me! I'll never even let you lick my boots!
HOLMES: You may leave, sir.

(*Le Biffon starts to exit.*)

WATSON: Is that wise, Holmes?
HOLMES: We can trace him and his mistress easily enough.

(*Suddenly, Liane de Pougy appears in the doorway.*)

LIANE: That will not be necessary, Monsieur Holmes. You see, I have come myself.
CAROLINE: Have you any business here, Liane? There are no stray men about, so you had best go back to walking the streets.

(*Liane enters. Her style is completely in contrast to Caroline's. Liane exemplifies a classical style. If we did not know her profession, we might take her for a virgin or a novice–she is dressed completely in white and wears no jewelry; her hands and neck are long, delicate, and aristocratic; her manners languid; her tone ironic and intellectual. For those who like their women refined, Liane is a far better choice than Caroline.)*

LIANE (*coughing slightly; her English, though accented, is educated, and clearly technically better than Caroline's pidgin, though perhaps not so racy*): Your abominable English climate has caused me a certain indisposition, Monsieur Holmes, but I shall give every satisfaction of which I am capable.

CAROLINE: *Vous voyez?* She never speaks but by double entendres. She always tries to seduce every man she meets.

LIANE: Hadn't *you* better go back to walking the streets, Caroline? I'm told the business is brisk in London. No doubt, with your appetites, you would be a sensation.

CAROLINE: *Elle est folle!* Me, a Grand Horizontal–the greatest Grand Horizontal in all the world, to walk the streets like a common whore!

LIANE: Control your temper, Caroline. *I* am the greatest courtesan in Paris, in France, and therefore, in the world–not you. You may as well resign yourself. You do not even have the advantage of youth, much less of taste or looks.

CAROLINE: Who will believe her? The woman is mad. The London fog has clouded her brain. Am I not the one they call the "Suicide Lady?"

LIANE (*dryly*): Doubtless, many men would consider suicide after fornicating with you. It surprises me that only two have so far acted on what must surely be a universal impulse.

WATSON: Ladies, ladies.

CAROLINE: In two years as a Horizontal, have I not made more money than any other Horizontal in history?

LIANE: Only by sleeping with more men than any respectable prostitute would dream of doing. Your industry, in this regard, while not to be emulated, is certainly remarkable.

CAROLINE (*angrily*): Ohhh! *Non!* It's because I'm the most beautiful! My legs are the toast of Kings.

LIANE: The Prince of Wales preferred these, Caroline. (*pulling up her skirt and stretching a beautiful, gartered leg forth.*)

CAROLINE: It's well known that he was near-sighted.

WATSON: Dear, dear, His Royal Highness.

LIANE: And the King of Belgium?

CAROLINE: An old goat. Why, with breasts like these, who would want you? Look at these beauties! (*she gives a little huff and pops her nipples loose from her gown*) Where have you seen beauties like these, M'sieur Holmès, in all your investigations?

HOLMES (*stupefied*): Ladies, I must ask you–

LIANE: On a cow! I'm sure that, while some men prefer overripe melons, men of discrimination, like Monsieur Holmes and Doctor Watson, prefer tastier fruit.

CAROLINE: Only men with no taste at all would eat off that table.

LIANE (*stung*): You overendowed cow! If you're such a great courtesan, why do you murder your lovers like some doxie from the gutter?

CAROLINE: Me! It's you who have murdered my gentlemen.

LIANE: Why should I do that when any man that has had you would be ready to commit suicide without much encouragement from me? Few like to contemplate death by prolonged disease.

CAROLINE: You, you, bitch! *Salope!* You, you're murdering them so that men will be afraid to love me, and because you can't get the good-looking men and the wealthy men away from me.
LIANE: I fancy they're afraid already, Caroline, with no assistance from me. No, it isn't I who's killing your lovers, Caroline, it's you.
CAROLINE: A likely story!
LIANE: Yes, you! You're killing them so as to acquire the reputation of a *femme fatale*–a reputation, which I might add, you could never achieve in any other way. Those two suicides of yours were comic.
HOLMES: Are you saying, Mademoiselle Pougy, that Mademoiselle Otero is murdering her companions simply to acquire a certain reputation, or notoriety?
LIANE: *Oui*, Monsieur Holmes. You see, in France, to be a prostitute, no matter how competent–and I'm willing to concede that Caroline is competent in that regard–is nothing. With us, in high society, style is everything. I have it, Caroline, poor creature, has not. Now, there are some men who like to play with fire, the Duke of Graustark, for example...
HOLMES: But why have you followed Mademoiselle Otero to London?
LIANE: Precisely to stop her from achieving her greatest goal: the seduction of the Duke of Graustark, who is about to become my lover. She knows he will soon be mine. The Prince of Wales and the King of Belgium have been my lovers. My crowning achievement would be the conquest of the Duke of Graustark. He isn't a King, but he is richer than the other two combined–and handsome, too. For months, he has thrown himself at my feet, but I have refused him.

CAROLINE: Refused him! Ha! I like to meet any man she has refused. Don't believe it, she is lying, *cette menteuse!*
LIANE: I am not.
HOLMES: Why have you refused such an opportune connection?
LIANE: You see, he isn't married, and being an absolute autocrat, there is nothing to prevent him from marrying me–which I expect he will do–therefore, I must refuse to become his mistress. Then, when these murders began, the Duke, who is, one must admit, a bit of a pervert, began to show some interest in Caroline. A very slight interest, purely from a romantic point-of-view for, you see, the Duke *loves* danger. Nothing else, I'm sure, could interest him in Caroline–except this, the knowledge that, if he becomes her lover, someone may try to kill him. That excites him as she never could. Talk about underhanded tricks.
CAROLINE: *Menteuse!* What a liar she is! The Duke has been courting me for months. You're trying to scare him away from me by killing my gentlemen. Well, it won't work. Arrest her, M'sieur Holmès! Take her to the Tower of London! *Tout de suite!*

BLACKOUT

Scene II

When the lights go up, Holmes and Watson are discussing the situation.

WATSON: What do you make of it, Holmes? I'm sure it's the strangest case you've ever been involved in.
HOLMES: It does present a few points of interest Watson–from a psychological point-of-view.
WATSON: I simply refuse to believe that either of those–those, er, ladies had anything to do with it.
HOLMES: Your chivalry does you credit, Watson–but if neither of them was actually involved, we seem to be without a suspect, or any usable clues.
WATSON: What a shame that two such majestic members of the fair sex should be ruined.
HOLMES: I doubt they regard themselves as ruined–
WATSON: It is especially terrible that such a delicate creature as Mademoiselle de Pougy should find herself in need of rescue–
HOLMES: Why, I believe you've taken a fancy to her, old man–
WATSON: Nonsense, nonsense. I was merely expressing a moral interest in her. She needs someone to protect her. I'm convinced she has a good heart and could be reformed–
HOLMES: I daresay that is the most utter sentimental drivel I have ever heard from you, Watson, and frankly I've heard a lot.
WATSON: Hmmph.
HOLMES: Soon you'll want to marry her–just to protect her, mind you–
WATSON: Now see here, Holmes–

HOLMES: I'm sure she'll bring a large dowry–
WATSON: Don't be so sarcastic. My impulses are pure in this matter. I'm interested in Liane from a purely–paternal–point-of-view.
HOLMES: Well, I shall best look for someone else to share rooms–I can see where this is leading.
WATSON: Hmmph. If you come to that, I think Caroline has a month's mind to you.
HOLMES: Are you mad? You know how I feel about women.
WATSON: Nonetheless, Holmes, I believe I observe these things a little better than you, for once. Caroline likes you.
HOLMES: Never!
WATSON: I'm sure she could be very persuasive.
HOLMES: I'll go to America first.

(*There is a jaunty knock at the door.*)

WATSON (*going to the door*): I wonder who that can be?
HOLMES: Well, open and we'll find out.

(*Watson opens the door and admits a flashily-dressed young man.*)

WATSON: Sir?
MAN: Ain'tchew Doctor Watson?
WATSON: I am.
MAN (*pointing with his cane*): Ain't he Sherlock Holmes?
WATSON: Yes, of course.
MAN: Glad to meetcha both.
HOLMES: The Duke of Graustark, I presume?

DUKE: Right-o. Howdja know that?

HOLMES: I've been expecting you for some time.

DUKE: Smart, aintcha?

HOLMES: Other than the fact that you've had three drinks, spent the afternoon with a woman, and have been listening at the door for ten minutes, I know nothing about you.

DUKE: You really are a corker, just like everybody says. That's good, I like interesting people.

HOLMES: I presume you've come because you think you are in danger?

DUKE: Oh no. Danger doesn't bother me. I like it, don'cha know?

WATSON (*stupefied*): Like it!

DUKE (*nonchalantly*): It relieves boredom. Boredom you see, is a kind of hereditary disease with the royal family of Graustark. Some royal families suffer from hemophilia or other interesting ailments, but we suffer from boredom.

HOLMES: Then it doesn't trouble you that someone may try to kill you because of your interest in Mademoiselle Caroline Otero?

DUKE: Not at all, don'cha know.

HOLMES: It has been suggested that Caroline is killing her lovers to attract you. What do you say to that?

DUKE: If Caroline is doing that just for me–it's kinda cute, don'cha know?

WATSON (*aside to Holmes*): I think they suffer from more than boredom in Graustark, and that is my professional opinion. This twit is feebleminded.

HOLMES: It has also been suggested that Mademoiselle Liane de Pougy has been killing Caroline's lovers just to scare you off.

DUKE: Well, that would be charming of Liane, too. All this just for me. Why, I might flatter myself in to thinking that I am rather a good catch.

WATSON: Could you seriously contemplate making a murderess your mistress?

DUKE: Well, I suppose it is a little unusual for conventional taste.

WATSON: Could you contemplate introducing such a woman to your mother?

DUKE: Oh–why they'd get along famously now you mention it.

WATSON: Surely, you jest.

DUKE: Fact. They could trade war stories.

WATSON: What on Earth do you mean?

HOLMES: The Duke means, dear Watson, that his mother is a very famous murderess.

WATSON: Really? The Queen Mother?

DUKE: Yes. Mama has a bad temper. Anytime she doesn't like somebody–well that's it.

WATSON: What do you mean?

DUKE: Mama poisons them.

WATSON: Good Heavens!

DUKE: Mama is a dear, really, but she's got a bad temper. She can't help it. Every member of the royal family has had a bad temper for the last four centuries.

WATSON: But, as Queen, why doesn't she just have people arrested?

DUKE: But that would be a misuse of royal power. Oh, no. I assure you, Mother has a very keen sense of propriety and justice. It would be wrong for the monarch to misuse her power by condemning her subject to death.

HOLMES: One has to agree to that.

DUKE: So how much more appropriate for mother to behave like a common subject and simply commit murder like anyone else would in the same situation.
HOLMES: Ah, the common touch.
DUKE: Exactly. That is why she has always been popular with the people. That and her sense of justice.
HOLMES: You do not seem to be troubled by the obvious danger to yourself or to Graustark.
DUKE: For myself, danger is something that relieves boredom. I have gone big game hunting in Africa. I have climbed the Himalayas. I have sailed the seven seas, as the saying is. One does what one can, but there are few lasting remedies for the disease in this humdrum century.
HOLMES: But you are a reigning autocrat. If you die, what will become of Graustark? What of the throne?
DUKE: I come from a large family, Mr. Holmes. I could easily be replaced. I have 26 younger brothers, several of whom, I must admit, could rule nearly as well as I do.
WATSON: Twenty-six. Your father must have been a strong man.
DUKE: Actually, I give more credit to Mama. You can understand why she has a bad temper I think. Papa wanted to have 27 but Mama refused.
WATSON: What happened?
DUKE: Father became very passionate about it, and threatened to divorce Mama for a woman who better understood her duty.
WATSON: Indeed? But he did not?
DUKE: No–he died rather suddenly. He should have known better than to make Mama angry.
HOLMES: Very thoughtless of him.
DUKE: Actually, it was Mama's most popular act as Queen.

HOLMES: I must still caution you. I believe you are in grave danger if you continue to associate with either Caroline Otero or Liane de Pougy.

DUKE: I cannot take your advice, Mr. Holmes. I only find women attractive who are dangerous in some way. Lulu the Lion-Tamer would only make love in a cage with her lion.

WATSON: I've heard of that woman. Didn't she kill herself?

DUKE: Yes, poor thing. She was very much in love with me, and couldn't stand it when I took up with the trapeze artiste.

HOLMES: How did she do it?

DUKE: She hung herself, poor thing.

HOLMES: Ah. Then your mother was not–

DUKE: Oh, no, no. Mama totally approved of Lulu.

HOLMES: And does she approve of Liane and Caroline?

DUKE: Certainly. Mother is very broad-minded. She doesn't care for respectable women. She thinks they're such bores.

HOLMES: Then you do not suspect your mother?

DUKE: Oh, no. Not her style at all. Strangling people is too crude. You see, my mother's line of the family descends from the Borgias.

HOLMES: What do you make of it, then?

DUKE: I think we can eliminate the Horizontals as suspects. Neither Caroline, nor Liane is behind this affair.

HOLMES: I am of your opinion, but I am at a loss for once to see where this leads.

DUKE: If I had my bet, I'd say it would be Baron Ollstreder.

HOLMES: Who is Baron Ollstreder?

DUKE: He is presently a lover of Caroline's. An odious, graceless–and shall I say it–boring–example of Prussianism. Very brave, I admit. Perhaps the greatest duellist in Europe, at swords or pistols. But as repulsive physically and morally as a toad.

WATSON: I wonder why Caroline has not mentioned this Baron.

HOLMES: Why do you suspect him?

DUKE: I rather fancy that murdering people is in his line. I have reason to believe that he is connected with German Intelligence and takes orders directly from the Kaiser.

HOLMES: What do you think he's up to? Why should he kill Caroline's lovers?

DUKE (*yawning*): No idea. Germans regard themselves as pretty deep, don'cha know. Actually, they don't know one word about espionage, but they must play their games. All I know is, he has much more money than he could possibly realize from the miserable little farm he calls a Barony in Prussia.

HOLMES: It seems to me, we must meet this Baron Ollstreder.

DUKE: I shall be happy to introduce you. We're great friends, of course.

HOLMES: When can it be arranged?

DUKE: I'm returning to Paris tonight. I thought it would be a lark to follow the ladies over. I knew Caroline planned to meet you, and I thought I might as well do that, too. You have an interesting profession, Mr. Holmes. Perhaps, I'll take it up. Perhaps, I shall be the world's first consulting Grand Duke. If I tire of being Grand Duke, don'cha know. Ta-ta. I'll let myself out, gents.

(*The Duke exits.*)

WATSON (*after the Duke has gone*): What a strange man.
HOLMES: We had best get ready to go to Paris by the night train, Watson.
WATSON: What do you make of it, Holmes? A rivalry between two of the greatest wh–scarlet women in the world. A Grand Duke with a mother descended from the Borgias. A German Baron who works as an agent for the Kaiser. Frankly, I can make nothing of it.
HOLMES: I wonder if the Grand Duke himself might be behind this.
WATSON: But for what reason?
HOLMES: Perhaps to relieve boredom.

(*Mrs. Hudson enters.*)

MRS. HUDSON: A telegram for you, Mr. Holmes. (*she gives him the telegram, and is about to leave.*) Who was that strange man who was here just now?
WATSON (*as Holmes reads the telegram*): That was the Grand Duke of Graustark.
MRS. HUDSON (*delighted*): A Grand Duke! Well, I never! In my house. Oh, if I'd only known!

(*She goes out.*)

WATSON: Well, Holmes?
HOLMES (*giving the telegram to Watson with a shrug*): Read it yourself.
WATSON (*reading*): "Dear Mr. Holmes: I've learned you are coming to Paris at the behest of Caroline Otero. If you are simply planning a lark for a few days in the

company of your charming employer, be welcome. But please do not meddle in my affairs, and especially those of the Grand Duke of Graustark. I should be most upset and the consequences might be very unpleasant. Fantômas."

CURTAIN

Act II

Scene I.
Caroline Otero's Apartment

A palatial and lavishly-furnished apartment in Paris. Caroline's taste is expensive, but gaudy. Holmes and Watson are escorted in by a servant. The servant bows and leaves.

WATSON: I say, Holmes, isn't this splendid!
HOLMES: Our client certainly has a lively sense of decoration.
WATSON (*examining an erotic drawing*): Good Heavens, Holmes–look at this!
HOLMES: Rather well-executed.
WATSON: By Heavens, Holmes, this is a picture of Caroline and...!
HOLMES: Why–so it is.
WATSON: This is disgraceful. Fancy, His Royal Highness posing for a picture like this.
HOLMES: I wonder what His Majesty would say, if he saw it?
WATSON: I prefer not to think of it. I must confess I'm rather shocked. As a patriotic Briton, I do not care to think of our King sneaking off incognito to Paris to associate with loose women.
HOLMES: Your sentiment does you honor, Watson.

WATSON: My respect for the crown will never be the same.
HOLMES: I am very upset with our client for not telling us about this Baron Ollstreder.
WATSON: The very name sounds sinister. Have you been able to learn anything about him?
HOLMES: Only that he is a very pugnacious duellist and seems to have lots of money.
WATSON: I suppose you must question Caroline.
HOLMES: I mean to, I assure you.
WATSON: By Jove, as a moral man I cannot approve of her profession, but I must say, this place becomes her mightily.
HOLMES (*dryly*): Your observations are improving, Watson.
WATSON: If results like these were generally known, it would be rather hard to preach chastity. It might destroy the whole moral order.
HOLMES: Fortunately, Watson, the English will never believe it.

(*Enter Caroline dressed as a Spanish dancer with castanets.*)

CAROLINE: Ah, M'sieur Holmès, Docteur Watson, at last, you have come.
HOLMES: We are delighted to be here–but I must chide you for not telling us about Baron Ollstreder. Why did you not advise me about him?
CAROLINE: Oh, it was what you call it?–an oversight.
HOLMES: A very significant one.

(*Enter Baron Ollstreder, a short, bald man dressed in a tuxedo. He comes directly towards Holmes and clicks his heels. He wears a monocle.*)

OLLSTREDER: I have the honor to introduce myself, Herr Holmes, I am Baron Adolf Ollstreder.
HOLMES: Enchanted, I'm sure. I have wanted to meet you for several days.
OLLSTREDER: I have the honor to advise you, Herr Holmes, to stay out of this matter, and to stay away from Caroline.
HOLMES: And if I do not?
OLLSTREDER: Then I shall be pleased to put a little bullet right between your eyes, Mein Herr.
WATSON: My dear Baron von Ollstreder, you must not think that an English gentleman will bow to pressure from a little Prussian bully.
OLLSTREDER: You will be willing to explain what that means, Herr Doktor?
WATSON: Of course.
CAROLINE: You will do no such thing, Adolf. Apologize to M'sieur Holmès and to the Docteur this instant, or never look at me again!
OLLSTREDER: *Ach*, Lina, I am only acting for your own good.
CAROLINE: This instant, apologize or get out. You cannot interfere in my affairs.
OLLSTREDER: I have never apologized to any man in my life. I am a Prussian officer.
CAROLINE: Now, Adolf! *Maintenant!*
OLLSTREDER: *Ach*, you do not understand that a Prussian officer cannot–
CAROLINE: Then, go! *Dehors!*

OLLSTREDER: Only for you, Caroline. Herr Holmes, Herr Doktor Watson, I apologize, but with the understanding that I would never do such a low thing except for love of Lina, and under duress.

HOLMES: Your apology is accepted as qualified, Baron.

WATSON: For this lady's sake, I accept your apology.

OLLSTREDER: Women are so unreasonable. I should much prefer to fight you, as becomes an officer and a gentleman, but, *ach*, I have a weakness for Lina–

HOLMES: I perfectly understand.

CAROLINE: Adolf has a very great friendship for me, M'sieur Holmès, but he is a little stupid. After all, he is a German–what can you expect?

OLLSTREDER (*laughs loudly, revealing a frightful pair of dueling scars that frame his face*): If a man said that to me, I would kill him. But I am an old man with a soft heart, *nicht wahr, liebchen?* (*He roars at this last remark, casting his head back and revealing a mouthful of gold teeth.*)

WATSON (*aside to Holmes*): It would be impossible to imagine a fellow more crude than this.

HOLMES: I am quite of your opinion, Watson.

OLLSTREDER (*putting his arm around Caroline in a crude gesture of possession, which Caroline ignores but in no way repulses*): Please understand, Herr Holmes, I am not afraid to cross swords or exchange shots with any man in Europe. I am under duress. I should be more than happy to take your measure. And I have heard you are very expert. It would be an honor I could not refuse.

HOLMES: I have no wish to prevent you from satisfying yourself, but I too am willing to bow to the wishes of this lady.

(*Ollstreder releases Caroline and steps towards Holmes; as he does so, Watson steps towards Caroline.*)

OLLSTREDER: Please understand, Herr Holmes, that I know of your courage and do not for one minute doubt that you or Doctor Watson would willingly fight me under other circumstances, and I appreciate your delicacy in this matter. I would especially appreciate your making no mention of this affair.
HOLMES: Certainly not.
WATSON (*to Caroline*): Let me tell him one word.
CAROLINE: What word?
WATSON (*passionately*): To keep his filthy Hun hands off of you.
CAROLINE: How nice of you, *mon cher Docteur*, but I forbid it. This is business.
WATSON: Your detachment under the circumstances is unbelievable.
CAROLINE: Money is money.
WATSON: You're too good for him.
CAROLINE: I've managed much worse. Besides, he might kill you.

(*She goes to Ollstreder and embraces him.*)

CAROLINE: The one perfect grace of this otherwise unappetizing old slop pot is that he never quibbles about such a contemptible thing as money. It's his one redeeming quality. (*She chucks him under the chin; Watson winces.*)
HOLMES: But I must ask you again, why you had not mentioned Baron Ollstreder to me, Mademoiselle?
CAROLINE: But Adolf has nothing to do with this affair. It is Liane. And besides, I hadn't seen Adolf for

some time. He only came round yesterday when he heard that Philippe had been so frightened that he has retired to the country for a few weeks.

OLLSTREDER (*contemptuously*): Just what you would expect from a Frenchman. A Prussian officer–a mere German for that matter–vould never disgrace himself so.

CAROLINE: Adolf, do not forget that I am a French citizen. I cannot allow such derogatory remarks to be made about my countrymen.

OLLSTREDER: You see what tyranny I live under, Herr Holmes? A man simply cannot speak his mind before this woman.

CAROLINE: Someday, Adolf, you will learn manners.

OLLSTREDER: *Ach!*

HOLMES (*to Caroline*): You do not think the Baron is in any danger, Mademoiselle Otero?

CAROLINE: *Mais non!* Who would dare to try to kill Adolf? He scares everybody. Just look at the brute.

HOLMES: And would a Prussian officer murder the lovers of his mistress so that he might have her all to himself?

OLLSTREDER (*frowning at first*): Were we not under a truce, there is only one way I should answer that question–however, as I must not quarrel with you, I will say truthfully that he might–if he did not prefer that his mistress have other lovers–*nicht wahr, liebchen?*

WATSON (*aside*): Let me kill him.

CAROLINE: Adolf is so perverted, M'sieur Holmès, you wouldn't believe it.

HOLMES (*dryly*): I think perhaps I should.

OLLSTREDER: I admit, Herr Holmes, I am capable of killing any man on the field of honor–but I scorn to strangle a man like a common murderer. *Ach!* (*He makes a gesture of contempt.*)

HOLMES: You are not jealous of Caroline's other lovers?
OLLSTREDER: *Ach!* For what, jealous? Let her have the best. It only makes me look better.
HOLMES: So vanity is at the root of your passion.
OLLSTREDER: Isn't vanity at the root of all passion, Herr Holmes?
HOLMES: Hmm!

(*Enter Liane, accompanied by Le Biffon, escorted by a servant who bows and withdraws.*)

CAROLINE: Liane? You here! What do you want?
LIANE: I have come to deliver a challenge to a duel.
WATSON: A duel!
LIANE: Yes, my dear Doctor, a duel.
HOLMES: But to whom is the challenge directed?
OLLSTREDER: Why, it must be to me, of course.
LIANE: It is hardly a challenge you could answer, my dear Baron.
OLLSTREDER (*puffing up like a cobra*): And why not?
LIANE: Because it is a battle between women. I am opening a new act at *Maxim's* tonight. I invite you to attend, Caroline. You shall have the best seats in the house. Come if you dare.
CAROLINE: I cannot refuse. It would be dishonor.
LIANE (*leaving with Le Biffon*): Now we shall see who is truly the greatest courtesan in France, Caroline. You will leave your pretensions at *Maxim's*.

(*Liane and Le Biffon exit.*)

WATSON: What do you make of it, Holmes?

HOLMES: I'm not sure, but I think we may expect significant developments tonight.
OLLSTREDER: We shall all go.
CAROLINE: You must excuse me, M'sieur Holmès. I must prepare myself for battle.

(*Caroline exits grandly, like a Valkyrie.*)

OLLSTREDER: I will shoot anyone who does not applaud Caroline.

(*He clicks his heels and exits, too.*)

WATSON: Before this business is over, that conceited little Prussian will answer to me. I believe he enjoys being disgusting.
HOLMES: Quite likely. Tonight offers some points of interest, Watson.
WATSON: I still don't see any motive for this.
HOLMES: I begin to think I see a little light–though it may be a false one. We shall know more tonight.

(*As Holmes and Watson are about to leave, a servant enters and offers Holmes a letter on a tray.*)

WATSON: What is it Holmes?
HOLMES: A letter, obviously. (*reading*) "Dear Mr. Holmes: Welcome to France. I am sorry I was unable to greet you personally, but certain circumstances temporarily make that impossible. You are in delightful company with Mademoiselle Otero, and I am sure she is more to your taste than I am. So enjoy Paris, enjoy Caroline, and do not meddle in my affairs. Fantômas."
WATSON: Fantômas again.

HOLMES: Yes, rather puzzling isn't it? And very suggestive.

(*Watson is about to reply when the Grand Duke enters.*)

DUKE: Ah, there y'are, old chap! Been looking for ya all over the place.
HOLMES: Indeed?
DUKE: Have a peek at this, will ya? (*handing Holmes another letter.*)
HOLMES (reading): "Dear Duke: I visited your hotel in your absence, and noticed you've brought several of the treasures of the Graustark Ducal Court with you. Item: A Leonardo drawing, two Titians and a Fran Angelico. As I wish to possess them, be so kind as to have them delivered to my friend, Baron Ollstreder, or I shall be obliged to come and take them myself tomorrow night. As these are priceless items, any offers I might make would surely be rejected as insulting, so I will merely take them to avoid offending you. I am consoled by the fact that the people of Graustark cannot miss these treasures as they were never allowed to see them. Fantômas."
WATSON: My God, Holmes!
DUKE: I wuz kinda hoping you'd help me with this, Mr. Holmes.
HOLMES (*hesitantly*): Yes, if I can. So It seems you have several masterpieces in your hotel?
DUKE: Yes, I'm very attached to certain paintings, so I drag them around the world with me. Apparently, this villainous Fantômas has somehow got wind of it...
WATSON: Don't you have security at your hotel?
DUKE: Supposedly, but apparently not enough to keep out this Fantômas chap. I so hope you'll help, Mr.

Holmes, because the people of Graustark do regard these paintings as national treasures, whether they've seen them or not. My mother would be especially upset and who knows what she might do then. And I would be very distressed as well.

                                        CURTAIN

Scene II
At Maxim's

We cannot see the stage. Holmes and Watson are ushered to a luxurious table. The orchestra is playing some Offenbach's Can-Can music.

WATSON: This place is magnificent, Holmes.
HOLMES: It has its reputation.

(*The music changes to sultry oriental music.*)

WATSON: I don't understand this show. *L'Araignée d'Or*. What's it about?
HOLMES: The Web of Gold, with Liane de Pougy. We shall soon see. Her act goes on in 15 minutes.
WATSON (*looking towards the stage*): I say, Holmes, that woman is taking off all her clothes!
HOLMES: A very observant remark, Watson.
WATSON: This show will be shut down by the Police.
HOLMES: Oh, no. The Police are very liberal-minded.
WATSON: Well, thank God this sort of filth doesn't go on in London. Holmes, will you look at that!
HOLMES: It might be better to observe the audience, Watson.
WATSON (*stupefied*): *She's doing it with a snake!*
HOLMES: Let's hope it's had its fangs pulled.

(*There is applause, catcalls, etc. Then a sudden hush.*)

WATSON: Why has everyone stopped?
HOLMES: Caroline is coming.

(*Caroline, in all her jewels, enters triumphantly like the Whore of Babylon, escorted by Baron Ollstreder. Amidst cheers from the audience, they go directly to the table where Holmes and Watson are seated. The two Englishmen rise and bow, then all are seated.*)

HOLMES: A remarkable entrance.
CAROLINE: Thank you, M'sieur Holmès.
WATSON: I think you have thrown down the gauntlet, Mademoiselle.
OLLSTREDER: Let Liane match *mein* Lina! Ha! Not possible.

(*The sultry music starts again.*)

WATSON: I say, Holmes, you really must look at this.
HOLMES: Really, Watson, it's quite elementary.
OLLSTREDER: *Ach*, what a nice, plump little woman.

(*Caroline slaps the Baron.*)

CAROLINE: When you are with me, Adolf, you do not look at other women.
OLLSTREDER: But, *liebchen*, I only said she looked nice.

(*Caroline pours a drink in his lap.*)

OLLSTREDER: *Ach!*
CAROLINE: *Cochon!*
WATSON: Holmes, is that not–can it be possible?
HOLMES: Indeed it is possible. It is David Renfrew.
WATSON: David Renfrew? It is Edward, the Prince of Wales.

HOLMES: That is the name he uses when he makes this sort of excursion.
WATSON: I say he's bowing to this table. Do you know him, Holmes?
HOLMES: Hardly. He's bowing to Caroline.

(*Caroline acknowledges the bow indifferently.*)

WATSON: I say, Mademoiselle Otero, that is no way to treat the Prince of Wales.
CAROLINE: That *petit garçon* simply does not know how to treat a woman like me. Let him go to Liane!
WATSON: As a patriotic Briton, let me say, Mademoiselle, that I am shocked the Prince, the heir to the throne, should frequent a place like this. And let me say, also, that I am shocked at the way the Prince is treated in a place like this.
OLLSTREDER: The Kaiser would never disgrace himself in such a way.
WATSON: Now see here, if that is meant as a reflection–
HOLMES: Not now, Watson. Look over there.
WATSON: Why, it's only an old man. What of him?
HOLMES (*whispering to Watson*): I think I begin to see the light.
WATSON: That's more than I can do. (*straining to look at the stage.*) Good God, Holmes. Can people actually do that?

(*There is a sudden hush as Liane enters. She is dressed entirely in white and sails by like a Princess. She wears but a single jewel, a large sapphire around her neck.*)

CAROLINE: Where is all her jewelry! Pitiful!

(*Trailing behind Liane, also dressed in white, is her black maid. She is bedecked with jewels, almost in imitation of Caroline. There is raucous laughter.*)

(*Caroline turns away in a fury, and sits with her face to the wall for a bit. Cries of "Liane de Pougy, notre courtisane nationale!" from the audience. It is obvious that Liane has won over Caroline.*)

OLLSTREDER: Only the French would bestow such a title on a woman. I'd like to see a German woman dare to call herself the "National Courtesan." We'd throw her in jail.
HOLMES: Doubtless.
WATSON: Isn't that the Duke of Graustark?
HOLMES: Yes. He's here.
CAROLINE (*to Ollstreder*): *La sale garce!* The filthy little bitch!
OLLSTREDER: *Ach*, Caroline. What can you expect from these French?
CAROLINE: I am French.
OLLSTREDER: *Nein, nein, mein liebe*, you are Spanish.
CAROLINE (*hissing*): I *am* French! Apologize!
WATSON: Liane is beginning her act.

(*The music changes and becomes more sultry and forbidding.*)

HOLMES: Quite so.

(*He is interested in the audience; Watson is fascinated by what's going on on stage.*)

WATSON: If you ask me, that costume is more suited to a harem than to the stage.
HOLMES: You're becoming quite a critic, Watson.
WATSON: That fellow who's part of her act is all tangled up in her web. What do you make of it?
HOLMES: Liane is playing the role of a spider. Men fall into her web and are caught. Silly, but effective.
WATSON: Ah, now I see. That fellow is doing a good imitation of Laocoon.

(*There is applause; the lights go down.*)

HOLMES (*suddenly excited*): Ah, that was interesting–
CAROLINE: So–you see it, too, M'sieur?
HOLMES: Pray what have you discovered?
CAROLINE: She is wearing falsies!

(*The lights go up.*)

HOLMES: Neither Mr. Renfrew, nor the Duke of Graustark are at their tables.
WATSON: Oh, is that all?
HOLMES: I have got to get backstage. Something is going to happen tonight–
WATSON: But how will you do it?
HOLMES: Can you make a diversion, Mademoiselle Otero?
CAROLINE: But certainly, M'sieur.

(*Caroline jumps onto the table, kicking over the glasses, and begins a wild gypsy dance, pulling up her skirts. At first, there is hesitation, then the orchestra starts to play* Carmen. *Two bouncers come over but the Baron jumps up instantly with his pistol out.*)

OLLSTREDER: The first person who dares to interfere, I will put a little bullet right between his eyes. Dance, *liebchen*, dance.

(*Caroline dances for several minutes. Then, Holmes returns, and she stops.*)

CAROLINE: How did you like that for a diversion, M'sieur Holmès?
HOLMES: It was so diverting that I nearly failed to profit by it.
CAROLINE: You find out something?
HOLMES: Only that Liane has apparently succeeded in making an assignation with both the Grand Duke and Mr. Renfrew for later this evening.
CAROLINE: What an alley cat! Why can't she be satisfied with one man at a time like me? You see what a respectable courtesan has to put up with? Absolutely shameless competition!
OLLSTREDER: *Ja, Ja,* Caroline–Liane should not work overtime like that.
HOLMES: Please excuse us, Mademoiselle, Baron. There is nothing more to be learned here tonight.
CAROLINE: I understand perfectly, M'sieur. You cannot stand to watch her any more, but you are too much the *gentilhomme* to say so, *n'est-ce pas?*
WATSON: If you don't really need me, Holmes, I, well, er–
HOLMES: I absolutely do need you, old fellow.
WATSON (*under his breath*): Damn my luck! (*aloud*) Why, of course, in that case–

(*They start to leave.*)

HOLMES: The game's afoot, Watson. We must be quick. The intelligence services of three countries are mixed up in this. I recognized Monsieur Lenormand backstage. He is the head of the French *Sûreté*–and maybe more, if my suspicions are correct. When I got backstage, I managed to slip into Liane's dressing room in time to hear her tell this fellow that she would see Mr. Renfrew first, then the Grand Duke in his hotel room.

WATSON: A strong woman, that. But what has this to do with Caroline and the murder of her lovers?

HOLMES: That, I cannot tell. But as loyal Englishmen, our duty is to see to the safety of the Prince.

(*Just as Holmes is about to leave, a waiter comes up to Holmes.*)

WAITER: I was asked to deliver this to you.

HOLMES (*taking the note and reading*): "Dear Mr. Holmes: You absolutely must not believe that I sent the telegram attributed to me to the Duke of Graustark. It is the work of an impostor, whom I will deal with. Fantômas. P.S. Rather interesting show tonight, wasn't it. Hats off to Liane."

WATSON: Fantômas was here! Tonight!

HOLMES: Evidently, but we must hurry if we are to accomplish anything.

WATSON: But what does it mean, Holmes? Who could be impersonating Fantômas, and why?

CURTAIN

Act III

Scene I
Liane de Pougy's Apartment

As richly furnished as Caroline's, but in a more modest, subdued taste. Enter Liane and Watson.

LIANE: It is very good of you to visit me, Doctor Watson, but it is very late.
WATSON: I am very sorry to disturb you, Mademoiselle, but I am to meet Holmes here.
LIANE: You may call me, Liane, Doctor.
WATSON: Thank you. You are very kind.
LIANE: You were present at my opening tonight, were you not?
WATSON: I had the pleasure of that experience, yes.
LIANE: Caroline, I fear, was not too pleased with my success.
WATSON: Her remarks, I fear, were not entirely objective.
LIANE: Perhaps, but they could be heard for several blocks.
WATSON: Actually, I thought your performance, while unsuitable for presentation in London–or in any part of Her Majesty's Domains, I am happy to say–nonetheless had a certain charm.
LIANE: You are too kind, Doctor.
WATSON: Liane–
LIANE: Yes, Doctor?
WATSON: Have you ever considered–?

LIANE: Considered what, Doctor?
WATSON: You shall think me very silly, but you are such a wonderful woman. Have you ever considered–changing your way of life?
LIANE: Oh, yes.
WATSON: I realize I'm just a stuffy old English doctor–but I think that, even though the French have different views about these things, that, well–
LIANE: You think I should reform, is that it?
WATSON: Well, yes, that is it, rather.
LIANE: You are certainly very sweet.
WATSON: You are not offended by my interfering?
LIANE: Certainly not. It means you like me.
WATSON: Well, as a matter of fact–
LIANE: So, how could I be offended?
WATSON: Then, you will consider–
LIANE: Some of the most interesting affairs I've ever had have begun just this way–
WATSON: That isn't quite what I meant–
LIANE: Are you sure? I have a great experience in these things and I can tell you that your type always starts off this way with a woman like me–
WATSON: My dear Liane, you misunderstand me–
LIANE: I don't think so, but of course, one must put one's ideas to the test.
WATSON: What do you mean by that?
LIANE (*moving in on him*): Would you like to kiss me?
WATSON: Now, see here!
LIANE: Or–if you are so shy–do you object to my kissing you?
WATSON (*retreating*): I wish Holmes would come. He'd know how to handle this! (*aloud*) Holmes will be here directly–
LIANE: Pooh! Let him wait.

WATSON (*retreating further*): The Lord is my Shepherd–
LIANE: You English men are so attractive, Doctor Watson. It's because you are so shy. You bring the Devil out in a woman–
WATSON: I think it's rather hot in here, don't you?
LIANE: Sometimes it gets positively torrid.
WATSON (*cornered*): Does it?
LIANE: Absolutely.

(*There is a loud rapping at the door.*)

WATSON: It's Holmes! Thank God!
LIANE: *Zut alors!*

(*Liane goes out and returns with Holmes.*)

LIANE: Well, Monsieur Holmes, you have arrived in the nick of time as you put it.
HOLMES: Have I indeed? You look rather distraught, Watson.
WATSON (*mopping his brow with his handkerchief*): Never better.
HOLMES (*to Liane*): Tonight, after your performance, I believe you went with the Prince of Wales to a *Maison* in town for a private dinner. You remained there until after he left.
LIANE: I am honored that you thought it worth your while to follow me.
HOLMES: I feared there might be an attempt on His Royal Highness' life.
LIANE: Surely, you were disappointed.

HOLMES: Pleasantly so. Shortly after His Majesty left, Baron Ollstreder arrived. He stayed for a few moments and then left. Watson followed the Baron.

WATSON: He went to the German Embassy and then to his own residence. Then I came here as you instructed me.

HOLMES: Shortly after the Baron left, Mademoiselle Pougy, you went to visit the Grand Duke of Graustark at his hotel.

LIANE: This is all quite true, Monsieur Holmes.

HOLMES: You remained with the Grand Duke for over an hour. Le Biffon accompanied you.

LIANE: A night in the life of a courtesan. Surely you must have something more than curiosity to cause you to follow me about like this? I slept with two men tonight, Monsieur Holmes. I am ambitious.

HOLMES: I am curious about what passed between you and Baron Ollstreder.

LIANE: You are much more clever than I thought. Indeed, you are a great detective. But I am not at liberty to disclose what passed between the Baron and myself.

HOLMES: You visited the Grand Duke on instructions from Baron Ollstreder.

LIANE: "Visiting" royalty is my profession, Monsieur Holmes. Unless you are a *voyeur*, I cannot see what interest this can be to you. (*coolly*) And I do not need instruction from Baron Ollstreder–nor do I take any–as to who I keep company with.

(*Enter Caroline, who pushes past the servant.*)

CAROLINE (*shrieking*): Murderess! Jealous bitch. Why did you kill him? Why?

LIANE: Are you drunk, Caroline? This is a respectable house, so please moderate your voice.
CAROLINE: You killed him! You killed him!
HOLMES: Mademoiselle Otero, you had best explain.
CAROLINE: Explain! *Bien sûr que je vais expliquer!* I have a rendezvous with the Duke of Graustark tonight. He sent for me to go to him at three o'clock. I go. What do I find? A dead Duke. And she killed him! (*pointing to Liane.*)
LIANE: Don't be absurd!
HOLMES: Did you leave him in good health?
LIANE: Quite excellent health, Monsieur Holmes. You might say he was in a state of bliss. It is my custom to leave men in such a state.
CAROLINE: You murdered him because he told you I was going to become his mistress!
LIANE: That is perfect nonsense.
CAROLINE (*shrieking*): Nonsense? Non, it's not nonsense! When I go to see the Duke, I have a key. I open the door. What do I find? The Duke, naked on his couch, tied up with this! (*She pulls out a golden sash.*) The murder weapon!
HOLMES: May I see that?

(*Caroline gives the sash to Holmes who examines it.*)

WATSON: Liane could not be guilty of this.
LIANE: Thank you, Doctor.
CAROLINE: She murdered him. It must be her. No one else. I believe it, I do!
HOLMES (*to Liane*): Do you recognize this cord?
LIANE: It is from the web I use in my act, of course.
WATSON: Think what you're saying, Liane!
CAROLINE: The Grand Duke was bound with this cord.

LIANE: But of course. I tied him up with it myself.
HOLMES: But why?
LIANE: He insisted. That is what he particularly liked. First, I tied him up, then I spank him with my slipper– so?
WATSON: You're putting your head in a noose.
CAROLINE: Then, you strangled him, *c'est ça*?
HOLMES: Did you leave him alive?
LIANE: Of course. Such activity rarely kills a man, though they often say they are dying.
CAROLINE: The Grand Duke was strangled with this cord. You admit you murdered him!
LIANE: Not by me. I suspect you, Caroline.
CAROLINE: Me? Me!
LIANE: Of course. You couldn't stand the thought that the Grand Duke was already mine.
CAROLINE: Liar! *Oh la menteuse!*
HOLMES: Did you find anything else of significance at the scene?
CAROLINE: Only this old circus ticket.
HOLMES: May I?
CAROLINE (*giving him the ticket*): Of course.
HOLMES: This ticket is five years-old.
CAROLINE: I found it next to the Duke's body. Ah, poor man, he loved me so much.
LIANE: *Merde!*
HOLMES: Do you recognize this ticket?
LIANE: It is from the *Cirque de Graustark*. Le Biffon!

(*Le Biffon enters. He had been hiding behind some drapes.*)

LE BIFFON: Yes, Madame.
LIANE: You used to be in the *Cirque de Graustark*?

LE BIFFON: Many years ago.
LIANE: You see this ticket?
LE BIFFON: *Oui*.
LIANE: What do you know about it?
LE BIFFON: Me?
LIANE: You.
LE BIFFON: Nothing.
LIANE: Do not lie!
LE BIFFON: I know nothing.
LIANE: You killed the Grand Duke.
LE BIFFON: Why should I do that?
LIANE: That is what I want to know.
LE BIFFON: Not me.
LIANE: You always follow me discreetly to my assignations, as is proper. You saw me leave, escorted me here, then went back and killed him. You left this ticket as some kind of calling card.
LE BIFFON: I see no reason why I should do that.
LIANE: I am asking you.
LE BIFFON: You better ask someone who knows.
LIANE: Le Biffon–
LE BIFFON: Madame?
LIANE: Untie my shoe.
LE BIFFON: *Oui*, Madame.

(*He kneels and, trembling, begins to untie her shoe; he is panting, his eyes bulge, his face is the color of eggplant.*)

LIANE (*pulling up her skirt a little*): Why did you do it?
LE BIFFON (*gasping*): I didn't do it.
LIANE: Le Biffon–
LE BIFFON: Madame?
LIANE: Who am I?
LE BIFFON: *Maîtresse...*

LIANE: Who are you?
LE BIFFON: *Votre esclave.* Your slave.
LIANE: Answer!
LE BIFFON: Because of Lulu the Lion-Tamer.
LIANE: Explain!
LE BIFFON: She was my sister. Five years ago, the Grand Duke seduced her.
LIANE: That's no reason to kill a man.
CAROLINE: Heavens no!
LE BIFFON: She loved him. When he went off with the trapeze artist, she killed herself.
CAROLINE: Romantic little fool! Kill oneself over a man! No, no! It is the men who must kill themselves over us!
LE BIFFON: I loved my sister very much. I wanted to kill the Duke, but, I couldn't get near him in Graustark. His protection was too good. So I left the Duchy and came to Paris. I worked for you. I tried to forget, but still, in my heart, I loved my sister. Then, tonight, I followed you as was my duty. I took you home then I went back. It was easy to get in; his bodyguard was asleep. I found him all trussed up like a turkey, with that gold cord. All I had to do was to tighten it up. I explained to him the wrong he had done my sister. He said he was very sorry, but then of course, I killed him.
LIANE: But you never thought of me. Didn't you realize I would be suspected?
LE BIFFON: I am sorry. I was so stupid. It was my big chance. I intended to take the cord, but I heard Caroline at the door, so I ran away.
LIANE: Stupid indeed! You should have killed her and made it look like a double suicide.
LE BIFFON: Next time, *Maîtresse*.

CAROLINE: But why did he kill Georges and Henri? What's Lulu got to do with them?
WATSON: That's a good point.
LE BIFFON: I did not kill those men.
WATSON: Then who did?
HOLMES: Why, Baron Ollstreder, of course. Please come join us, it must be dark behind those curtains.

(*The Baron emerges, pistol in hand, from behind the curtains.*)

OLLSTREDER: You are quite right, Herr Holmes.
HOLMES: You see, Watson, the Baron was trying to prevent Caroline from interfering with Liane.
CAROLINE: You, Adolf? You love me so much you have to kill everybody else?
OLLSTREDER: Caroline, if you had not been such an idiot, none of this would have been necessary. You see, Herr Doktor, we had to restrict Caroline's activities a little. Caroline could not be recruited to our service. You can get gossip out of her easily enough, but she will never agree to work for anybody. A shame, too, because she has lots of opportunities. Several of my agents approached her, but they were rejected with indignation.
CAROLINE: I should think so! *Moi*, a Grand Horizontal, stoop to spying. Never!
OLLSTREDER: So, what to do? The Grand Horizontals are sleeping with all the Kings, Ministers, Grand Dukes and Bankers of Europe. They get all kinds of information. Liane was smart. She agreed to work for us, but Caroline was always trying to snare the same Kings, Ministers, Grand Dukes and Bankers... What to do? Leave it to German ingenuity. We cannot harm a

woman. So we kill off Caroline's lovers and frighten everybody else into Liane's arms. Clever, *nicht wahr*?
HOLMES: And you get to keep Caroline to yourself, in the bargain.
CAROLINE: *Ça alors!* I'm sure this was Liane's idea.
HOLMES: Diabolical! Almost worthy of Moriarty.
OLLSTREDER: Who?
HOLMES: The Napoleon of Crime.
OLLSTREDER: *Ach*, we defeated him at Waterloo. Anyway, I have to kill you, and Herr Doktor Watson too, now. Then, I'll kill Le Biffon with your gun. Everybody will think you killed each other, and Le Biffon will be blamed for murdering everybody.
LE BIFFON: You're going to kill me, too? I don't like that.
OLLSTREDER: Yes, and Caroline, too, unfortunately.
LIANE: That's a better idea. Start with her.
CAROLINE: Adolf, you cannot!
OLLSTREDER: I can. But I will leave you till last. First, I must kill Herr Holmes.

(*Watson tenses and is about to rush the Baron.*)

LIANE: *Quel dommage!*
OLLSTREDER: Please step aside, Liane, and plug your ears.

(*The Baron points his pistol towards Holmes. Watson starts to rush him, Caroline shrieks, and a shot rings out.*

The Baron collapses at Watson's feet. Liane blows the smoke away from her derringer and returns it to her gown. Holmes has not moved an inch.)

WATSON (*examining the Baron*): You have put a bullet right between his eyes.

LIANE: The only thing I regret about killing that wretch is that he left everything in his will to Caroline.

CAROLINE: *C'est vrai?* How much do I get?

WATSON: Then you are not working for the Germans?

LIANE: Me? The National Courtesan of France work for the Boche! I'll have you know that my father was a French Officer! Do you think that, because I am a courtesan, I am not also a patriot? (*placing her hand majestically over her heart*) When the Tricolor flies, does not my heart beat a little faster, like any French woman?

HOLMES: Allow me to introduce you to the best agent in the employ of the French *Sûreté*, Watson.

WATSON: You knew all along, Holmes?

HOLMES: I had a brief discussion with the gentleman I told you I recognized–Monsieur Lenormand.

LIANE: You were very brave, Doctor Watson.

WATSON (*bowing*): Thank you, Liane.

LIANE: It was time to write *finis* to the Baron's activities. We had been feeding him false information for several years. Indeed, German Intelligence knew just about what we wanted them to know–which was not much, and most of it misleading. But we owed them for killing two of our agents in Berlin recently. This will be but a small installment on that debt. The good Baron will have to take the responsibility for murdering the Duke of Graustark, too. That will certainly cause our German friends a good deal of embarrassment.

HOLMES: And who will be responsible for the Baron's death?

LIANE: Why, you and Doctor Watson, Monsieur Holmes. I'm sorry, but that is the price you must pay for my saving your life.

HOLMES: I have a better idea.

LIANE: What is it?

HOLMES: Let's blame it all on Fantômas.

LIANE: On Fantômas? That's an amusing idea. But how?

HOLMES: Fantômas has been sending me letters. We met a few years ago under circumstances I'm not at liberty to reveal. This is his latest: "Dear Mr. Holmes: Sorry that we are unable to meet again, but pressing business prevented me from renewing our acquaintance. By now, you will have realized that the Grand Duke of Graustark was planning to secretly sell copies of the masterpieces belonging to the Grand Duchy under the pretext that I, Fantômas, had stolen the originals. I was alerted to his ingenious scheme by an art collector, who is also a customer of mine. I then realized that someone was appropriating my good name and reputation. It didn't take me long to deduce that only the Grand Duke himself would have the audacity to impersonate me, or to supervise the forgeries. He had been behind several similar swindles in order to revive the Duchy's finances and support his womanizing, gambling and extravagant lifestyle. While I greatly admired his ingenuity, I thought it was quite outrageous for him to involve me in his sordid schemes. Besides, I stand behind everything I steal and would never offer forgeries for sale. So, as revenge, and to redeem my good name in my customer's eyes, I have gone to Graustark and taken the original artworks in question. I will deal with the Grand Duke himself as soon as I return to Paris. Fantômas."

WATSON: The Duke was selling forgeries of the Graustark collection! Why, that's abominable!

LIANE: Very ingenious–and this letter will make it easy to pin the Duke's murder on Fantômas! But what about Ollstreder?

HOLMES: In the Fantômas letter the Grand Duke forged (*he gives it to Liane*), he referred to Ollstreder as his friend. It was a crude joke, but we shall make use of it. We shall say they were in cahoots, then had a falling out and Fantômas killed him. I saw him do it, didn't you, Watson?

WATSON (*stupefied*): Why, yes, I did, if you say so.

HOLMES: And then he left as suddenly as he came.

WATSON: Why, so he did. But won't this make the real Fantômas furious?

HOLMES: I doubt it; more likely, he'll be grateful. But I'm sure we shall hear from him again–soon.

WATSON: But–

HOLMES: You seem reluctant, Watson.

WATSON: We'd be lying.

HOLMES: That's true.

LIANE: After all, it is the least you can do. I had to break my cover. Surely, you will not object to saving a lady from minor embarrassment?

WATSON (*bowing*): I should be delighted.

LIANE: As for Le Biffon, we shall forget about Lulu. He really is quite helpful and we must overlook this little indiscretion. After all, it's not likely to be repeated.

CAROLINE: And what about me? You think I am going to let you get away with this, Liane? Now, I don't have any more gentlemen!

LIANE: My dear Caroline, you will certainly find someone else easily enough. And the Baron left you nearly half a million pounds in his will. He was fond of you, the disgusting old goat. That should be enough to silence you. If not, we shall have to accuse you of spying for the English and the Russians.

CAROLINE: Me! Never! I never spy for nobody. *Jamais!*

LIANE: It really doesn't matter if the accusation is true or not. If we have to, we'll prove it, even if we have to forge the evidence.

CAROLINE: Lies! This is blackmail!

LIANE: Exactly. So do keep quiet about all this. And from now on, Caroline, you will also have to work for us. Is that clear?

CAROLINE: Very well. But I call on M'sieur Holmès to witness that I am under duress.

LIANE: If you like. Now that this is all settled (*pushing the Baron with a little slippered foot*) I think the exertion has been too much for me. I think I have palpitations. Do something, Doctor.

(*She falls into the arms of the astonished Watson.*)

HOLMES: Well, don't just stand there. Watson, attend to your patient. Le Biffon and I will attend to the Baron.

(*Watson leads Liane off.*)

LE BIFFON (*picking up the Baron's body*): I shall put him in the cellar till morning. I don't need any help.

(*Exit Le Biffon.*)

CAROLINE: Humph! This is a fine mess you created! Now I must work for Liane. We have both had Kings, Dukes and Millionaires for lovers. Poets, playwrights and sportsmen have fallen at our feet. In everything, I have been her equal, but that is not enough. (*pausing, she looks directly at Holmes*) But I shall be the only Grand Horizontal to have slept with the World's Greatest Consulting Detective.

(*Holmes wraps his cape about him and flees without a word.*)

CAROLINE: Don't go, *Chéri*. I'll prove to you who is the greatest courtesan in all the world.

(*She exits running after him.*)

BLACKOUT

Scene II
Liane de Pougy's Cellar

A dark, foreboding place, with cobwebs, a wine rack, etc. There is a big trunk against a wall and a small, high window leading into the night, outside.

(*Le Biffon enters, dragging the Baron's body behind him. He abandons it unceremoniously on the ground.*)

LE BIFFON (*in a voice much more refined and quite unlike his previous accent*): I said I would deal with the Grand Duke and I'm always true to my word.

(*He grabs his face and pulls it off–it was a mask! Underneath is a black cowl with only two slits for the eyes.*

He goes to the chest and opens it. The real Le Biffon is inside, all tied up. With a knife, Fantômas frees him.)

FANTÔMAS (*for it is he*): If you know what's good for you, my friend, you won't say a word about this. Bury that German and let's this remain our little secret. Ha! Ha! Ha!

(*Still laughing, Fantômas, moving stealthily like a panther, goes out through the high window.*)

CURTAIN

Epilogue

221B Baker Street

WATSON: I never expected you to quit the field of honor so precipitously.
HOLMES: There is a time for everything, Watson. That was definitely not the time for heroism. I regard that as the single most close call I have ever had, not excluding that little incident with Professor Moriarty at the Reichenbach Falls.

(*Enter Mrs. Hudson, a rather dumpy little woman dressed all in black.*)

MRS. HUDSON: Mr. Holmes, so you have returned at last.
HOLMES: Ah, my dear Mrs. Hudson.
MRS. HUDSON: Don't you "my dear Mrs. Hudson" me.
HOLMES: But Mrs. Hudson–
MRS. HUDSON: I fear Mr. Holmes, I shall have to give you notice.
HOLMES: But, I have paid my rent–
MRS. HUDSON: You have had a woman up here in my absence. I never thought a gentleman like you would be capable of such a thing especially when my back was turned.
HOLMES: My dear Mrs. Hudson, I assure you–
MRS. HUDSON: Now, don't you be trying to fool me, sir. It was a French whore. I am something of a detective myself in these matters. No, sir, it will not do. The only

business she was here for was monkey business. Not in my house.

(Watson and Holmes try to protest as the

CURTAIN FALLS.

The Adventure of Merlin's Tomb

(*Sherlock Holmes and Father Brown*)

Characters

Sherlock Holmes, a consulting detective
Dr. Watson, his roommate and confidant
Father Brown, a Roman Catholic priest
Father Sebastian, another, older priest
Mrs. Hudson
Dr. Abell
Mrs. Carbury
Nurse (Abigail Lang)
Old Woman (Mary Good)
A Gypsy
An infant in swaddling clothes
Six men, three women

The story takes place around 1896, in a small Cathedral town somewhere in Essex.

The set should be very abstract. No effort should be made to actually change scenes. In particular, the Rectory and the interior of the Cathedral should be joined. If possible, part of the stage should represent Baker Street. Center stage, the Cathedral and stage right, Dr. Abell's home/surgery.

Those areas of the stage not being used should be darkened.

Scene I
221B Baker Street

Holmes and Watson are involved in a heated discussion. Watson is very upset. Holmes, as usual, imperturbable.

WATSON (*heatedly*): Holmes, my dear fellow, you are endangering your reputation.
HOLMES: What is reputation to the advancement of science, Watson? (*snapping his fingers*) I don't give that for my reputation.
WATSON: But, what are you about, Holmes?
HOLMES: I am trying to perfect a method of reconstructing the human face from the skeleton alone.
WATSON: And that is why you've been going to Bart's and measuring the faces of corpses with calipers?
HOLMES: Precisely. Before and after dissection.
WATSON: All the doctors are commenting on it.
HOLMES (*lighting his pipe, amused*): Not favorably?
WATSON (dejectedly): Not favorably.
HOLMES: But, don't you see how important this discovery is? To Criminalistics?
WATSON: But I've read several studies that say it is not possible.
HOLMES: True, Watson. I read those studies, too. And I became convinced they are based on certain false premises–not to mention an inattention to detail. Now, do as I do. Pinch the skin on your cheeks and pull the skin away from the bone as far as you can. (*doing so.*)
WATSON (*imitating Holmes rather clumsily*): Very well.
HOLMES: Now, here. (*moving the site of the pinch.*)

WATSON (*imitating Holmes*): All right.
HOLMES: Do you observe the skin is thicker in some places than others?
WATSON: Well, yes, but what of it? Everyone knows that–
HOLMES: No, everyone does not know that. Now, if you will observe, when I pinch–

(*Enter Mrs. Hudson with a small, rotund young man in the habit of a Catholic priest.*)

MRS. HUDSON: A visitor for you, Mr. Holmes. Ha, ha, ha. You both look so funny.
HOLMES (*not embarrassed*): All in the interests of science, my dear Mrs. Hudson.
MRS. HUDSON: Whoop! A scientific undertaking. Making faces at each other like children. Ha, ha, ha–you are too droll, Mr. Holmes, ha, ha, ha.
WATSON (*irritated and terribly embarrassed*): What is the name of our visitor, Mrs. Hudson?
MRS. HUDSON: A Romish priest, I believe. And his name is Brown. (*whispering to Watson*) But, I don't believe it, not one word. And in my house. A papist.

(*Exit Mrs. Hudson, laughing and muttering.*)

BROWN: Mr. Holmes, I believe? My name is Brown.
HOLMES: I am pleased to meet you, Father Brown. This is my colleague Dr. Watson.
WATSON: Delighted. I think we should explain to Father Brown that the situation in which he found us is subject to misconstruction and that–
HOLMES (*lightly*): I'm sure Father Brown understands–
WATSON: And, that we are not in the habit of–

BROWN: Oh, there's no need for explanations.
WATSON: Of making fools of ourselves–and, that–
HOLMES: How can we be of service to you, Father Brown?
BROWN: Well, I'm not sure I ought to have come here, but, frankly, I'm at my wits' end, and I can't see the bottom of it.
HOLMES: Please, tell us what has happened.
WATSON: And, that we were, in fact–
BROWN: It's my lack of experience, I'm sure. Otherwise, I should have known what to do. You see, I was only recently ordained, and my first assignment was to a small and quite ancient parish in Essex. I was ordered by my superiors to examine and report on the archives of the Church. They go back to the time of the Conquest. The only point of interest is that they refer to the existence of an ancient tomb located somewhere in the Church.
HOLMES: Most interesting. And the Church is very ancient, too?
BROWN: Parts of it probably date from Roman times. It has been rebuilt several times. Most recently, about 30 years ago.
WATSON: And the tomb has never been discovered?
BROWN: It was discovered about a month ago. Some alterations were being done to repair damage caused by a small fire that occurred before I was posted there. It was then that all the trouble started.
HOLMES: What trouble?
BROWN: Within a week of the discovery of the tomb, the Verger hanged himself–at least the Coroner's jury thought it was a suicide. A mortal sin for a Catholic, and almost unheard of in the clergy.
HOLMES: To be sure. Is this all?

BROWN: Last week, the Dean apparently went out of his mind. He was found in–I believe the medical term is a catatonic state.

WATSON: Dear me. This is strange.

HOLMES: Pah! A coincidence. What connection can there be?

BROWN: We have no idea–except that there is some. If this were not enough to fan the flames of superstition, yesterday, the wife of one of our oldest parishioners began manifesting signs of demonic possession.

HOLMES: Come, come. In the 19th century?

BROWN: The woman is nearly 80, and I find it difficult to describe what she was doing–she was soliciting men to sexual intercourse, amidst the most shocking blasphemies.

HOLMES: Needless to say, rumors have begun to fly about a curse on the tomb. The usual drivel.

BROWN: Exactly. Merlin has been seen at night. The usual nonsense. An exorcist has been sent for.

WATSON: Please, I don't understand–what has Merlin got to do with all this?

BROWN: There's a local tradition that Merlin was buried hereabouts.

WATSON: Is there really? Most extraordinary.

BROWN: Part of the reconstruction involved removing the pulpit to give a clearer view of the altar. When this was done, the sarcophagus was found. It bears the image of a rather fierce-looking old man. There is nothing to suggest from the scant ornamentation that he was a Christian. I have tried to put a name to him, but I cannot.

WATSON: Could it really be Merlin? I've always been fascinated by Merlin, since I read Tennyson's *Idylls of the King*. This is indeed exciting, Father Brown.

HOLMES: But, however extraordinary these events are, Father Brown, they appear to stem from natural phenomena.

BROWN: You do not believe in demons–demonic possession, Mr. Holmes?

HOLMES: Certainly not. Although some silly people may think themselves possessed and act accordingly.

BROWN: And, the demons themselves?

HOLMES: Not at all.

BROWN: As a Catholic, I am obliged to believe in demonic possession as a fact.

HOLMES: Then, undoubtedly, you have made the correct choice in seeing assistance from an exorcist.

BROWN (*decisively*): Not in this case, Mr. Holmes. Fiends are at work, but they are human fiends.

HOLMES: Then, you attribute it to human–

BROWN: To human sinfulness, Mr. Holmes. I have certain suspicions about the person or persons behind these events–but I am too inexperienced to trust my own judgment.

HOLMES: In that case, you seek the type of assistance I can offer?

BROWN: Most definitely, Mr. Holmes.

HOLMES: Well, then, tell us exactly why you think these events are related.

BROWN: First of all, they happened within a short period of time.

HOLMES: Pah! Coincidence.

BROWN: Secondly, they have all happened to people who are quite aged. The youngest person was 72.

HOLMES: Inconclusive. And thirdly?

BROWN: Thirdly, there are certain elements of witchcraft connected with each of the incidents.

HOLMES: Witchcraft! Really, Father Brown. I thought we had dismissed that sort of explanation.

BROWN: Oh, no, no, Mr. Holmes. I never said witches weren't involved–I only said demons weren't involved. These witches are quite human and have been practicing their loathsome rites for upwards of 50 years.

WATSON: What, in the 19th century? In England? Not 50 miles from London? Impossible!

BROWN (*unruffled*): I have the most unshakeable proofs. After the Dean became incapacitated, it fell to me to arrange his belongings. It was while doing this, that I found a cache of hosts.

WATSON: Hosts, Father Brown?

BROWN: Consecrated wafers. You understand their function in Catholic ritual, Dr. Watson?

WATSON: I believe I do, but what is so strange–?

BROWN: An orthodox Catholic priest does not keep them wrapped in a purple cloth, hidden in a chest with his private belongings.

HOLMES: Interesting. Why would he keep them, then?

BROWN: They are sometimes used in performing a Black Mass and other abominations. After I found them, I examined the Dean's personal effects much more closely.

HOLMES: And you found?

BROWN: A Satanic Bible, also wrapped in purple silk– together with a kind of diary.

HOLMES: Have you examined the diary?

BROWN: Carefully. It suggests a motive for the events– or, at least a connection–although there's still a mystery to it.

HOLMES: I will need to see the diary.

BROWN: I brought it with me. (*giving the diary to Holmes.*) You see, it contains a careful record of Black

Masses and other abominations going back nearly 50 years.

WATSON: I find that incredible. Surely, it is some sort of hoax.

BROWN: I wish it were. The Black Masses have been recorded in exquisite detail. Every abomination and sacrilege that is conceivable has been practiced. Even human sacrifices.

WATSON: Human sacrifices! It must be a hoax.

BROWN: Human sacrifices have taken place in Derbyshire, on the very altar of our beautiful Cathedral.

HOLMES: There can be no mistake in interpreting these passages, Father Brown. It appears quite authentic.

WATSON: Good Heavens, Holmes. Human sacrifices! How awful!

HOLMES: The rituals were repeated as often as twice a year, it would appear. The participants in these orgies are identified by what appear to be code names. The leader of the cult is called Merlin. Have you any idea who is intended?

BROWN: No. I think, however, we can be sure the Verger, the Dean, and Mrs. Carbury–the old woman who is propositioning old and young alike–are clearly members.

HOLMES: Some elements of conclusive proof are lacking, but I believe your supposition is correct.

BROWN: From what I have been able to puzzle out from the diary, the Dean was admitted to the cult soon after he became a priest. He was not, however, the leader. All of the cult members are local people, I believe. And they have been practicing their wickedness for over 50 years.

HOLMES: Then, they must all be quite aged.

BROWN: These are not just parlor Satanists, Mr. Holmes. They are not just engaging in the thrill of attending a Black Mass and rubbing shoulders with the Devil. Oh, no, they are very scrupulous, almost pious in their satanic devotions.

HOLMES: Are all the members of the cult alive except the Verger?

BROWN: The diary never records a death, but eventually some names cease to appear and never recur– as has happened several times in recent years.

WATSON: But, what is the connection between these events and the discovery of the tomb?

HOLMES: Ah, there, my dear Watson, lies the key to the mystery. Well, a strange game is afoot. What do you say to a journey to Derbyshire, my dear fellow?

                                                         BLACKOUT

Scene II.
The interior of the Cathedral in Derbyshire

The reconstruction is evident. In the center, near the altar, is a tomb. The features of a rather ferocious-looking old man are carved on it. Holmes, Watson, Father Brown and Father Sebastian enter, in conversation.

HOLMES: A most beautiful little town.
WATSON: Impossible that such a lovely English town could be the site of such unholy goings-on.
SEBASTIAN: That's exactly what I think. I refuse to believe that any of my parishioners could be guilty of such a thing. Right under my nose. No, it is, as you say, impossible. There's some other explanation.
WATSON (*to Holmes, in a whisper*): About the right age for Merlin, don't you think?
SEBASTIAN (*a little deaf*): Merlin–yes. They say it's his tomb.

(*They all go to the tomb.*)

BROWN: A more unchristian countenance I have never beheld. There is evil about this tomb.
SEBASTIAN: I think we should cover it up again.
HOLMES (*examining the tomb*): The lid could hardly be lifted with less than three or four men, without heavy machinery. There is no sign that it has been disturbed in decades past. (*pacing up and down*) Frankly, I'm puzzled.

BROWN: There is a connection, Mr. Holmes. I'm certain of it.
HOLMES: And I am, too. But, for the life of me, it eludes me what it may be.

(*Dr. Abell emerges from the shadows.*)

ABELL: Perhaps, you believe in ghosts, Mr. Holmes? That would no doubt solve the mystery.
BROWN: Ah, Dr. Abell. How are your patients?
ABELL: Well, I am not too concerned about the Dean. But, Mrs. Carbury is failing. I have put her under heavy sedation.
SEBASTIAN: Dr. Abell is our leading physician–and my brother.
ABELL: The only physician–and, therefore, the leading physician, Mr. Holmes. I've practiced here for nearly 50 years. Unless, Dr. Watson is planning to set up as my rival–
WATSON: My dear sir, I assure you–but, how do you know my name?
ABELL: Oh, my brother keeps me well informed.
HOLMES: I should like to visit your patients, Dr. Abell.
ABELL: Very well. Come after dinner. They are at my home, which serves as a sort of hospital. I won't give them any more sedation. I will prepare them.

(*He goes out.*)

WATSON: A very impressive man.
SEBASTIAN: I wish he weren't such a misanthrope. But, he is really very kind. He has practiced here all his life, when he could have done well in London. He is attached to Derbyshire–as I am, for that matter.

BROWN: He is a very capable doctor.

HOLMES: May we see where the Verger hanged himself?

SEBASTIAN: I suppose you may as well... But, on reflection, I think, perhaps, better not. There is no reason to involve you in this matter. It is a Church matter.

BROWN: But, you object even to summoning an exorcist.

SEBASTIAN: It's all a mistake, a misunderstanding. The Dean is of a literary turn. I am sure when he regains his reason, there will be a satisfactory explanation. Probably writing a novel.

BROWN: It is a Satanic Bible–

SEBASTIAN: Nonetheless–

HOLMES: Perhaps, we should eliminate the possibility that a crime has been committed. Where did the Verger hang himself?

SEBASTIAN (*reluctantly*): He hung himself from the Cross behind the altar.

(*Holmes goes to the altar and looks around.*)

HOLMES: Well, the Verger was definitely murdered.

SEBASTIAN: But, how can you tell that? The Coroner's jury said it was suicide.

HOLMES: There's a good deal of dust back here from the reconstruction. There are the footprints of three men, coming in from the side near the rectory. They stopped here. Two of them carried the third man to the Cross, and left the way they came. One of the men was very tall.

BROWN: But, how do you tell that?

HOLMES: From the length of the stride.

SEBASTIAN: But, why couldn't those be the footprints of the men who rescued him?
HOLMES: The footprints of the rescuers are apparent, too. They come from in front of the altar. They cut him down, and laid the body here, to the right.
BROWN: That's so, Mr. Holmes. I was one of the persons who found him. It happened exactly as you say.
SEBASTIAN: Dreadful, dreadful. I withdraw my objection. Murder must be investigated by the civil authorities. It is not simply a Church matter.

Scene III
Dr. Abell's residence-hospital

Holmes, Watson and Father Brown enter.

WATSON: Wasn't that a gypsy woman we saw as we came in?
BROWN: Yes. I wonder what she wanted with Dr. Abell?
WATSON: Probably begging.
BROWN: Oh, no, these gypsies never beg. They come here once or twice a year, around Christmas or Easter– for no apparent reason. But, they never beg, or cause any trouble. But, for all their good behavior, somehow, I don't like the looks of them.
HOLMES: Beautiful flower garden. It appears to be much better taken care of than the rest of the grounds.
BROWN: Yes. A rather odd flower garden.

(*Enter the Nurse, an old woman with a peasant accent.*)

WATSON: We've come to see Dr. Abell. He's expecting us.
NURSE: He is with the Dean. The poor man be failing fast.
HOLMES: We must hurry, then.

(*Enter Dr. Abell, wringing his hands.*)

ABELL: I'm afraid it's no use, Mr. Holmes. The Dean is dead. His last words were, "Merlin. Beware Merlin." Surely, this Merlin nonsense is catching.

HOLMES: I thought you said there was no need to worry about the Dean, Dr. Abell?

ABELL: So I did. He'd been improving, though his reason was sadly gone. About an hour ago, he went into convulsions. I administered several drugs, but to no avail. It happens that way sometimes.

WATSON: I've seen it often enough myself. The patient will progress well for some time, and then suddenly, for no apparent reason, he's gone.

HOLMES: And he spoke of Merlin? He wanted to communicate something?

ABELL: Which proves conclusively his delirium. What would he know about a man who, if he ever lived, has been dead a thousand years?

BROWN: It may have been important.

ABELL (*laughing*): Oh, that it must. We all want to know about Merlin. Perhaps, you care to see my other patient? Maybe she can inform you about Morgan le Fay, and King Arthur, too.

HOLMES: Yes, I'd like to see her. At all events, there is nothing more to be learned from the Dean.

BROWN: I must administer the last rites to the Dean.

(*Exit Father Brown with the Nurse.*)

ABELL: By all means. But, I do not care to observe. Mr. Holmes, I will escort you to see Mrs. Carbury. She is, I fear, hopelessly mad.

(*Enter Mrs. Carbury, in a disheveled condition.*)

MRS. CARBURY: Someone to see me. I like visitors.

ABELL: You should have remained in bed, Maria. But since you are up, so be it. This is Mr. Holmes and Dr. Watson. They wish to ask you some questions.
MRS. CARBURY (*winking coyly*): I like questions.
HOLMES: Who is Merlin, Mrs. Carbury?
MRS. CARBURY: Merlin—why, he's a devil.
ABELL: You'll get nothing out of her.
HOLMES: When was the last time you saw Merlin?
MRS. CARBURY: Why, I see him now.
HOLMES: Why did the Verger hang himself?
MRS. CARBURY: Hang him—hang him—good for him, he deserved it!
ABELL: Perfectly useless.
MRS. CARBURY: Come closer, Dr. Watson, and I'll tell you about Merlin and John the Baptist, too.

(*Watson approaches and, as she seems about to whisper in his ear, she grabs him by his privates and kisses him!*)

MRS. CARBURY: Fuck me! Fuck me! Quick, Watson! Be a man to me.
WATSON (*pushing her off with disgust*): Be off, woman!
MRS. CARBURY: Don't be shy, Dr. Watson. I like shy men. Fuck me!
ABELL: That's enough, Maria. (*holding her and forcing a sedative on her.*)
MRS. CARBURY: I'll show you the best time you ever had.
ABELL: Be a good girl.
MRS. CARBURY (*the sedative taking effect, beginning to weep*): Ahhh, ahhh, ahhh!

ABELL: That's better. First Merlin, now John the Baptist. Saint Peter next, ha, ha! I'm afraid, Mr. Holmes, you'll learn nothing from either of my patients.
HOLMES: I fancy we have already learned a good deal.

                              BLACKOUT

Scene IV
The Rectory

WATSON: Brr! I can still feel her lips on mine. It was like embracing a corpse.
BROWN: Another brandy, Dr. Watson?
WATSON: Please. (*drinking it off quickly.*) What do you make of it, Holmes?
HOLMES: I think we have confirmed that both the Dean and Mrs. Carbury were part of the witch cult.
WATSON: How so, Holmes?
HOLMES: Both talked of Merlin. In Mrs. Carbury's case, she also referred to John the Baptist.
BROWN: And John the Baptist is a name used in the diary to refer to one of the warlocks.
HOLMES: In the original coven, there were six witches and six warlocks, as the diary shows. (*hands around a list*) I've made up a list of the names and indicated on what pages of the diary they are mentioned.
BROWN: The names themselves are an affront to God.
WATSON: What do the dates mean?
HOLMES: If I am correct, the date indicates the last date at which the named person was present at a meeting of the coven.
BROWN: If so, then not more than six were alive at the date of the last entry.
HOLMES: That seems likely. Have you noticed anything else that seems suggestive?
BROWN: Yes. The witch Ishtar stopped coming to meetings long before the rest. About 30 years ago. The rest died off within the last five years.
HOLMES: Exactly, Father Brown.

WATSON: But, of what use is such information?

HOLMES: Derbyshire is a small parish. If all the members of the coven are local residents, we ought to be able to determine the names of some of the deceased members of the coven, simply by checking the parish register. That, in turn, may give us some clue as to the names of the living members.

BROWN: There is another point, Mr. Holmes. The early death of the witch Ishtar may be significant, too.

HOLMES: You are very perceptive, Father Brown. What made you notice that, and what significance do you ascribe to it?

BROWN: The diary hinted in Aesopian language of human sacrifices. They appear to occur around the dates of significant Christian rituals. Easter, for example. Usually it would seem that children are intended.

WATSON: Children! How abominable.

BROWN: But, an entry for the year 1866 suggests an adult female was sacrificed. That was also the year in which we hear the last of Ishtar.

HOLMES: And you think Ishtar was the victim?

BROWN: Undoubtedly.

HOLMES: If you could check the parish register for 1866.

BROWN: I already have.

HOLMES: Splendid! And, what have you found?

BROWN: Absolutely nothing. No woman over the age of ten died in 1866 or 1867.

WATSON: Perhaps the death was not reported.

HOLMES: Yes, of course. We must try to determine if any one was reported missing. If our theory is not in error, something must turn up for that year.

WATSON: Why place so much emphasis on discovering the identity of someone who died 30 years ago?

HOLMES: Morbid curiosity, perhaps, dear fellow. But, in fact, her death is a key to the mystery confronting us.

WATSON: I should think it would be more important to locate living members of the cult.

HOLMES: All in due time. Is it not very suggestive that the recent events should all occur after the discovery of the sarcophagus a few weeks ago?

WATSON: Yes, but I'm not sure what it suggests, unless you give credence to some supernatural power or curse.

BROWN: Evil will out.

HOLMES: Yes, it will. Even after 30 years. Apparently, in 1866, a member of the witch cult was sacrificed. If the death of Ishtar raised no questions in the community, then for some reason the disappearance must not have been noted. Did you not say the Church was remodeled in 1866 or 1867?

BROWN: Yes, indeed. According to the records, the pulpit was rebuilt, and extensive changes were made in the interior.

HOLMES: Who supervised the rebuilding?

BROWN: The Dean, I believe.

HOLMES: And, who is superintending the present remodeling?

BROWN: That task was given to me. In fact, the Dean was quite upset about so junior a person as myself being placed in charge. But, Father Sebastian was adamant.

HOLMES: We must open that tomb. There is more than archeological evidence to be found. I'm certain of it.

BROWN: I think the three of us could lift that slab.

BLACKOUT

Scene V
The Rectory, later that night

Holmes, Watson and Father Brown enter. Holmes removes a skull from a sack and places it on the table. The skull has several clumps of long blond hair clinging to it.

HOLMES: I think we were able to replace everything.
WATSON: There's no doubt the woman in the tomb was murdered. She had a jeweled dagger in her ribs.
BROWN (*examining the dagger*): I think the dagger explains why the Dean was so nervous. It has his initials on it.
WATSON: What shall we do now, Holmes? Call the Police?
HOLMES: This is too serious a matter to confide to the Police. I fear we are no closer to discovering Merlin. If the Dean murdered Ishtar–or performed the sacrifice, if you will, there seems nothing in the way of physical evidence to connect the murder to Merlin, or to help us in identifying him.
WATSON: But, why did the Verger commit suicide?
HOLMES: He didn't. Remember? The Verger was murdered. I think the Dean became nervous and communicated his fear to the Verger. The Verger was then silenced, perhaps by the Dean, but more likely by Merlin. Disposing of the Verger was a temporary solution. The Dean knew the tomb would eventually be opened and remained fearful he would be called to account.
BROWN: And suffered a breakdown.

WATSON: But, how does that account for Mrs. Carbury?

HOLMES: Mrs. Carbury was probably close to the Verger or the Dean. What happened to them unhinged her.

BROWN: But, Merlin and the others are alive and well– and believe that nothing can connect them, with either the tomb or the fate of the Verger.

HOLMES: And rightly so, Father Brown, for unless new evidence comes to light, we are at an impasse.

BROWN: That is dreadful, Mr. Holmes. Because Easter is approaching.

HOLMES: At the rate things are going, I doubt we shall solve the puzzle before then.

BROWN: But we must, Mr. Holmes, we must.

HOLMES: There is no urgency. Religion will not suffer if the solution is put off beyond that date.

BROWN: But a male child will.

HOLMES: What do you mean?

BROWN: Is it not apparent that child sacrifices have been performed by these witches in the past? Is it not likely that they will kill again, as is their custom?

WATSON: Good Heavens, Holmes! We must do something.

HOLMES: I don't know what we can do. My powers only carry me so far.

BROWN: I think we must resort to a stratagem.

                                            BLACKOUT

Scene VI
The Rectory

WATSON: What a sermon Father Brown gave! If that doesn't smoke the witches out, nothing will. Why, I almost believed he knew everything, and I know he knows no more than we do.
HOLMES: Father Brown is a remarkable man. I suspect the other witches don't know that the Dean kept a diary, or what was in it.

(*Enter Father Brown.*)

BROWN: Now, we shall see what effect that will have.
HOLMES: I think we may expect an attempt on your life, as soon as Merlin can decently arrange it.
BROWN: Yes. I expect that.
HOLMES: Watson and I will give you what protection we can.
BROWN: I trust God.

(*Enter Father Sebastian.*)

SEBASTIAN: There you are, Father Brown. I must reprimand you. I may have to suspend you.
BROWN: What is wrong, Father Sebastian?
SEBASTIAN: You know very well what is wrong. Did you not, in your sermon, imply that things had been revealed to you in confession about witchcraft?
BROWN: I did just that.
SEBASTIAN: Need I remind you of your duty as a priest? Confessions must never be revealed. I will have

to suspend you, and report matters to the Archbishop for his decision.

BROWN: That's unnecessary, Father Sebastian.

SEBASTIAN: Why? That's the correct procedure.

BROWN: I didn't receive the information in confession. I lied.

SEBASTIAN: You lied about a thing like that?

BROWN: It was necessary. We hope it will frighten the witches into taking some precipitous action. Nothing that I said in my sermon was revealed in confession.

SEBASTIAN: Oh, in that case, I can absolve you myself. A hundred Hail Marys!

BROWN: I would never reveal anything I learned in confession.

SEBASTIAN: I should hope not. Oh, I almost forgot to tell you, I was so upset. Dr. Abell says that Mrs. Carbury is dying. He thought you would want to administer the last rites.

BROWN: I do. I'll go at once.

HOLMES: Before you go, perhaps you would like to look at Ishtar as she once was. (*unveiling the head.*)

SEBASTIAN (*gasping*): Why–why, it's Jennie McPherson!

HOLMES: You know this woman, Father Sebastian?

SEBASTIAN: Why, yes. Jennie McPherson was a seamstress. She eloped some 30 years ago, and no one has ever seen her since. She was from Scotland, of course, and had no relatives here.

HOLMES: She never left Derbyshire.

SEBASTIAN: How can that be, Mr. Holmes?

HOLMES: You are looking at the real Jennie McPherson, or I should say, her reconstructed face. Her skull was removed by me from Merlin's tomb last night.

She was a member of the witch cult, and herself a human sacrifice to Satan.
SEBASTIAN: She was a member of the choir when I was choirmaster. She was a good girl, even if she was a little wild. I feel very sick, Mr. Holmes.

(*Father Sebastian exits.*)

HOLMES: I wonder if there was something between Jennie McPherson and Father Sebastian?
BROWN: It's not uncommon for a celibate priest to have strong feelings for a pretty parishioner. Now I recollect, he once told me that he fell in love with a woman, but God intervened, and she went away. Well, I had best go see Mrs. Carbury.

BLACKOUT

Scene VII
Dr. Abell's residence-hospital

Holmes, Watson, Father Brown and Dr. Abell are talking.

BROWN: Thank you, Mr. Holmes. I fear they might have been too much for me, if you had not come along.
HOLMES: Were you able to get a good look at them?
BROWN: Unfortunately not. But, they were young men, Mr. Holmes, neither was over 30.
WATSON: I found this.
HOLMES: A gypsy bandana.
BROWN: Gypsies must have attacked me.
ABELL: Those gypsies are up to no good. First thing in the morning, I'm going to the police, and have them notified to be gone. They've moved altogether too close to home for comfort. They should be on their way immediately. You've had a narrow escape, Father Brown. Pray be more careful. I don't want to lose all my patients.
BROWN: I'll be all right. If we hurry back, I'll be in time to hear confession.

BLACKOUT

Scene VIII
The Rectory. Late night

Watson is snoozing in a chair. Pebbles are thrown against the window. Watson starts, takes his revolver, opens the window. A tall angular gypsy enters through the window.

HOLMES: No, no, Watson.
WATSON: Holmes, I almost didn't recognize you.
HOLMES: Where is Father Brown?
WATSON: I don't know. He left suddenly, without a word to anyone. I think he's a bit daft. He kept muttering about Dr. Abell's garden–said it was unnatural, evil. Catholicism does strange things to people.
HOLMES: He's gone. Hmm. That's not good. But, we don't have time to concern ourselves with him. The witches mean to hold a Sabbath tonight in the Church. We must conceal ourselves immediately.
WATSON: Is it possible? But, how do you know? And, why are you disguised as a gypsy?
HOLMES: All in good time, Watson. We must hurry before the witches get here. Shh–get down.

(*Enter Father Sebastian. He lights a candle and places it before the altar. After praying briefly, he goes out. Holmes makes no move.*

The street door opens and two old women come in. They carry bags. As soon as they are in, they quickly remove quantities of black crepe and cover the windows with it. Then, they drape the altar in black and position the

Cross upside down. They begin to dance around the altar.)

WITCHES: Merlin, Satan, Lover. Come to me.

(*The street door opens, and a man enters. He changes clothes briefly in the shadows. He wears a purple robe with a golden sash. On his head is a goat mask. He holds a golden chalice and advances towards the altar.*)

MERLIN: Great Master Satan, we, your worshippers, will offer you sacrifices this night.
WITCHES: Reward your servants.

(*A knock at the street door. Merlin opens the door, and receives a little child from a man dressed like a gypsy. He takes the child to the witches, who make cooing noises over it.*)

WITCHES: What a pretty baby. Such a good little thing. Soon, you will be with Father Satan.
MERLIN: Lead the sacrifice to the altar. (*raising the knife over the child.*) Master Satan, receive this sacrifice from your humble servants.

(*Holmes leaps forward.*)

HOLMES: Now, Watson!

(*Holmes rushes at Merlin, and a furious struggle ensues, counterpointed by a more comic match between Watson and the Witches. Merlin is getting the better of Holmes, while Watson subdues first one, then the second witch.*)

MERLIN: Now, Sherlock Holmes, I will sacrifice you to my master.

(*Father Brown enters from behind and strikes Merlin a terrific blow on the head with a shovel. Merlin collapses.*)

HOLMES: Your assistance is very welcome, Father Brown. But, how did you get here?
BROWN: I was at Dr. Abell's house, investigating his garden. I saw him leave and I followed him here. I entered from the Rectory.
HOLMES (*regarding the prostrate masked Merlin*): So, it is Dr. Abell.

(*One of the Witches gets up and starts to flee, but Watson grabs her, and soon ties her up with some crepe.*)

WATSON: Ah, would you?
HOLMES: Do you know these women? Abigail Lang, Dr. Abell's housekeeper, and Mary Good, a woman with a reputation for great piety and devotion.
HOLMES (*removing Dr. Abell's mask*): I believe Dr. Abell is dead.
WATSON (*examining him*): Yes. Stone dead.
BROWN: A shovel is a handy weapon against the Devil.
HOLMES: What made you suspect him?
BROWN: I didn't suspect him. I suspected his garden. The place reminded me of a cemetery. There was something wrong about it. I went digging there tonight. Someone had already dug a shallow trench on one side. One doesn't do that in a flower garden.

HOLMES: The trench was probably intended to receive the remains of tonight's sacrifice.

BROWN: It looked like a grave, but it was too small for a man. It looked more as if it were for a child. Then, I thought of the child sacrifices. I dug around a little bit, and it wasn't long before I found an infant's skull. When I saw the Nurse and Mrs. Good leave the house, followed shortly by Dr. Abell, I concealed myself and followed them here. But, how is it that you came to be here, Mr. Holmes?

HOLMES: Why, it was the gypsies, Father Brown. I remembered your saying they always show up in the vicinity around Easter and Christmas. If the witches were sacrificing children, they had to get them somewhere. Obviously, they were not taking local children, or people around here would have been aroused. They must be getting them somewhere else.

BROWN: Yes, of course, I should have realized that myself.

HOLMES: It was very suggestive that the gypsies caused no trouble and soon left. Obviously, they were on their best behavior, and trying to make themselves inconspicuous. They must have some reason to do that, because most places they go, they either beg or panhandle. Then, of course, they figured in the attack on you. The deduction was elementary that the gypsies were stealing the children from afar and selling them to the witches here.

WATSON: But, why are you dressed like a gypsy, Holmes?

HOLMES: I went to the gypsy camp earlier tonight. Keeping in the shadows, I was able to mingle and overhear enough to learn they intended to deliver the child to the Church this very night–and break camp at dawn. When I learned the exchange was to take place at the Church, I reasoned a Black Mass was scheduled.

WATSON: I shall never feel the same about burning witches again. They most richly deserve it.

HOLMES (*looking at the tomb*): I wonder if this really is Merlin's tomb?

BROWN: We shall probably never know, but one thing is certain. Merlin was no more dreadful than his latter day namesake.

WATSON: We had better see about getting these witches to the Police.

(*Suddenly, the baby that has been lying on the altar cries.*)

HOLMES: Well, we seem to have nearly forgotten the child. Will you play Nanny, or shall I?

CURTAIN

The Adventure of the Mulberry Street Irregular

(*Sherlock Holmes and Teddy Roosevelt*)

Characters

Sherlock Holmes, a consulting detective
Dr. Watson, his roommate and confidant
Police Commissioner Theodore Roosevelt, President of the Police Board of New York City
Lincoln Steffens, a young reporter
Professor Moriarty
Mrs. Laura Avery
Dr. Parkhurst, a Reform Minister
Parker, a member of the Police Board
Clubber Williams, a Police Inspector
Schmittberger, another Police Inspector
Police Chief Byrnes
A Police Officer

The story takes place in New York in 1896.

Scene I

A hotel room in New York occupied by Sherlock Holmes and Dr. Watson. Holmes is in a funk.

WATSON: We've been cooped up in this bloody hotel room for several weeks, Holmes. Are you sure that Professor Moriarty is in New York?
HOLMES: I'm positive he's here, Watson.
WATSON: But why would he come to New York anyway?
HOLMES: To keep out of my way.
WATSON: Well, he's certainly gone to ground. Have you lost the scent?
HOLMES (*piqued*): It appears, Watson, we must simply await developments. Moriarty will announce his presence in some spectacular way. The man cannot be idle. Sooner or later, he will pull off some criminal coup.
WATSON: He seems to have managed to restrain his impulse so far.
HOLMES: He's prudent. He's hoping I'll get tired and return to England. He underestimates my patience and his own need for action.
WATSON: Well, I propose an excursion tomorrow while we wait for the Professor to give some evidence of his whereabouts.
HOLMES: A capital idea, Watson. We may as well mix business with pleasure. At least until we can profitably do business.
WATSON: I think it most inconsiderate of Moriarty to come to New York and then hide so cleverly.

HOLMES: What better place than New York, Watson? The city is filled with people of all kinds and the government is so corrupt that even the Police can be bought.
WATSON: Yes, I've been reading about that. Well, there's a Reform Movement afoot.

(*A knock at the door. Holmes gets up and opens the door, admitting Lincoln Steffens, a reporter.*)

STEFFENS: Mr. Holmes, I presume?
HOLMES: I am Sherlock Holmes and this is Dr. Watson.
STEFFENS: Of course. I should have recognized both of you instantly. I follow your adventures very closely as reported by the good doctor.
HOLMES: I have not the same pleasure of knowing you, sir.
STEFFENS: My name is Lincoln Steffens. I'm a reporter.
HOLMES: With the *Evening Post*?
STEFFENS: That's right. How did you know?
HOLMES: I've been reading your accounts of the reform of the Police. Quite excellent work.
WATSON: Indeed, I've read them too.
STEFFENS: Some people say it's muck raking. I appreciate your praise.
HOLMES: Unfortunately, Mr. Steffens, I do not grant interviews to the press.
STEFFENS: Ah, but you see, I am not seeking an interview, although I should be glad enough to have one.
HOLMES: Indeed. Then, of what service can I be to you?

STEFFENS: The President of the Police Board requested that I contact you.
HOLMES: Mr. Roosevelt? But I am engaged in the most urgent business at the moment.
STEFFENS: Are you pursuing Professor Moriarty?
HOLMES: How could you know that?
STEFFENS: What else would bring Sherlock Holmes to New York City? We don't have any master criminals.
HOLMES: You are certainly a very clever and engaging young man. I venture very few men in America have ever heard of Professor Moriarty.
STEFFENS: The President of the Police Board has heard of him.
HOLMES: This Theodore Roosevelt must be a remarkable man.
STEFFENS: He is, indeed. And, he is willing to offer you the assistance of the NYPD in apprehending Moriarty, if you would assist him in a small matter.
HOLMES: I generally do not work well with the Police, Mr. Steffens.
STEFFENS: Neither does the President of the Police Board, Mr. Holmes.
HOLMES: I shall be delighted to meet the new President of the Police Board, and be of what service I can. But, I must warn you, that it is unlikely that I can devote much time to any other endeavor than the pursuit of Moriarty.
STEFFENS: The President understands your position, Mr. Holmes. He is willing to put his entire resources behind you, and to be of every assistance he can in your great enterprise. It could save you a lot of time.
HOLMES: Still, Police methods–
STEFFENS: The NYPD may be corrupt, Mr. Holmes, but they are among the world's finest.
HOLMES: I mean no slight.

STEFFENS: Then, allow me to present Mr. Theodore Roosevelt, President of the Police Board.

(*He goes to the door and admits T.R., who bustles in, cigar in mouth, flashing his teeth.*)

STEFFENS: He asked me to make the introduction.

T.R.: Holmes, Watson, welcome to New York. Good to see you, good to see you. We must get down to business right away. You must solve this mystery for us, Mr. Holmes. Meanwhile, I will undertake to put every available man on the lookout for Moriarty, and furthermore–

STEFFENS (*amused at the somewhat aghast expression on the face of Holmes*): The President of the Police Board and the future President of these United States, T.R.!

T.R.: Now stop that, Steffens. I've told you before, I won't have that, even in jest.

STEFFENS: Certainly not, President Roosevelt. President Roosevelt has the theory that he must do his present job with absolutely no thought of the future.

T.R.: Without fear or favor. And stop calling me "President."

STEFFENS: I was referring to your position on the Police Board. Anyway, Mr. Holmes, he fears that if he thinks about the future, he will beat himself.

T.R.: Steffens is the most incorrigible, impudent fellow I've ever met–which is why he's just about the best reporter that ever lived–saving Jake Riis, of course. And he has the damnedest ideas about human nature, too. Would you believe it, Mr. Holmes, he convinced me to

keep the bag man for all the crooked cops on the take, because he says, mind you, that he's an honest man?
STEFFENS: Schmittberger is honest. That's why Tammany trusted him with the payoff money.
HOLMES: Isn't this Schmittberger the one who testified at the Lexow Commission and turned State's evidence?
T.R.: He's the man. And you know what, he really is honest. He never kept a penny of that money for himself.
HOLMES: Yes. And he kept very precise records of the officers he paid money to.
WATSON: You mean this Schmittberger is still on the force?
T.R.: And I mean to keep him there. I've put him in charge of reforming the department. He knows who was on the take.
WATSON: Well, it couldn't happen in England.
STEFFENS: It was the system that corrupted Schmittberger. He hated the system, and now he'll be loyal to us.
T.R.: He can be depended upon to clean out the grafters and to close down the saloons, the gambling dens and the whorehouses. I'd never have thought of that, if it hadn't been for Steffens.
HOLMES: I begin to have a high opinion of you, Mr. Steffens.
T.R.: It's really Schmittberger we've come to see you about, Mr. Holmes. We think he's in great danger.
STEFFENS: He's received threatening letters.
HOLMES: Surely, that's to be expected after his testimony implicating so many of his fellow officers and Tammany Hall.
STEFFENS: These are different in tone.
T.R.: They've begun to worry him, and it's affecting his work. (*giving Holmes some letters.*)

HOLMES: They appear to have been pasted together from newspaper print.

STEFFENS: As a matter of fact, I think they're from the *Evening Post*. It looks like our style to me. Unfortunately, we enjoy a wide readership.

HOLMES: "Enjoy your sleep, Schmittberger. It may be your last. Did you hug your kids tonight? It may be your last chance. Death is near. Obacht." Obacht, what does that mean?

STEFFENS: It's German slang. It means watch out.

HOLMES: You speak German, Mr. Steffens?

STEFFENS: Fluently. I was educated in Germany, Mr. Holmes.

HOLMES: These letters offer little of real interest. The man who wrote them has a gift for saying things that are disturbing and designed to hurt the reader. Beyond that, I would think your best bet is to put on a mail cover. Pure Police work, that.

T.R.: Except, that the Police cannot be trusted in this case. That is why we came to you as soon as we found out you were in town.

HOLMES: Do you have any individual suspects?

STEFFENS: Clubber Williams.

HOLMES: And, who is Clubber Williams?

T.R.: He's a Police Inspector. He's famous for his brutality with a nightstick. Hence the nickname Clubber.

STEFFENS: To be blunt about it, the man's a sadist.

HOLMES: Any others?

STEFFENS: Well, the present Police Chief, James Byrnes.

WATSON: Why, doesn't this Chief Byrnes enjoy a great reputation as a detective?

STEFFENS: Almost equal to that of Sherlock Holmes. But he got it by cheating.

WATSON: Got what by cheating?
STEFFENS: His reputation for solving cases. You see, he lets the criminals operate so long as they don't cause too much trouble. Say you had your pocket picked, and you're an influential person. You go to Byrnes. Byrnes says, "Don't tell anybody. I'll have your stuff back in a week." And a week later, you get your stolen goods back. You think Byrnes is a master detective. But, what really happened. He calls in the leading pickpockets and says he wants such and such an item back. The pickpockets get together and find out who took it and tell him to give it back.
WATSON (*naively*): But, why should they give it back?
STEFFENS: Because, if they don't, Byrnes will make it hot for all the pickpockets in the city.
HOLMES: The ancient Egyptians had a system like that. You could buy back your stolen property.
T.R.: We haven't progressed much. Police protection should be available to everyone. Not just to those citizens who have influence.
HOLMES: Any other suspects?
STEFFENS: Tammany Hall, the saloon-keepers, the proprietors of the gambling dens and the brothels–and last, but not least, the entire Police Department.
WATSON: Hmmph. No end of suspects.
T.R.: Mr. Holmes, if you would give me a description of Professor Moriarty, I would circulate it immediately.
HOLMES: That is perfectly useless.
T.R.: Why? Don't you know what he looks like?
HOLMES: I know him very well. He is tall, thin and emaciated-looking. I can only say that you will never see him like that. He is a master of disguise. Look for a short hunchback of decidedly stupid appearance and you will have your Moriarty.

(*Enter Inspector Schmittberger; a tall, impressive looking officer.*)

T.R.: Schmittberger, what are you doing here?
SCHMITTBERGER: They told me you were here, sir.
T.R.: What has happened? You look upset.
SCHMITTBERGER: A man on a bicycle fired two shots at me as I was leaving O'Banion's Saloon.
T.R.: Were you hit? Did you get him?
SCHMITTBERGER: No, sir, I wasn't hit. But, a bystander was killed. I didn't get him. The killer got away.
HOLMES: How do you know the assassin was after you?
SCHMITTBERGER: He yelled at me. He called me a dirty stool pigeon and then he fired. This other poor chap was killed instead, poor devil.
T.R.: Did you get a look at him?
SCHMITTBERGER: Not a good one. He was around the corner almost immediately. I got my gun out, and ran after him, but he was lost in the crowd.
HOLMES: Do you have any idea who was trying to kill you?
SCHMITTBERGER: Some of the boys said they'd get me for turning State's evidence. But, I told them to come ahead. Let them come at me, fair and square. Even Clubber Williams is no match for me. I'll beat them all, and they know it.
HOLMES: Are you sure it wasn't one of the Police?
SCHMITTBERGER: I'd recognize any man on the force. I've never seen that man before. He was a total stranger.
T.R.: A killing for hire.

HOLMES: Who was the man killed?
SCHMITTBERGER: A business man who frequents O'Banion's for lunch. I've seen him there many times.
T.R.: It would appear he might have better chosen to dine elsewhere.

                                        BLACKOUT

Scene II

Roosevelt's office at Police Headquarters in Mulberry Street. The floor around Roosevelt's desk is covered with paper. Roosevelt is talking with Holmes, and reading a memo at the same time. As soon as he finishes the memo, Roosevelt balls it up and tosses it over his head where it ends up in the same pile. Holmes and Watson look on, somewhat aghast.

T.R.: No doubt, you find Mulberry Street a contrast with Scotland Yard, Mr. Holmes.
HOLMES: I seldom frequent the Yard.

(*Roosevelt demolishes another memo, disposes of it rapidly, and picks up another.*)

T.R.: I hate paperwork.
HOLMES: Yes, I've noticed.

(*Enter Dr. Parkhurst, a small bearded clergyman, accompanied by Steffens.*)

PARKHURST: Steffens said I could see you, even though you were with someone, Mr. Roosevelt.
T.R.: Ah, Dr. Parkhurst, you know you can see me any time. This is a pleasure. Allow me to introduce you to Sherlock Holmes and Dr. Watson. You've heard of them, I am sure.
PARKHURST: Yes, indeed. Very glad to meet you, Mr. Holmes, and you, Dr. Watson. We need a man like you in this city. Unfortunately, there are few mysteries

worthy of your famous abilities. All we need really is a new broom—a man who will enforce the law.

STEFFENS: Dr. Parkhurst is the backbone of the Reform Movement.

HOLMES: Indeed, I've heard of your exploits, Dr. Parkhurst. Is it not unusual for a clergyman to take such a concern in the suppression of crime?

PARKHURST: God announces his mission in strange ways, Mr. Holmes. It started when I began a youth group in my church. Young men. After a while, they told me they were having a hard time living Christian lives because of all the temptations they were exposed to. I said what temptations? And they told me all about the saloons, and whorehouses, and the whole lot. I was naïve. These places were illegal. I went to the Police and asked that these dens of iniquity be shut down. It took me quite a while before I realized that these places enjoyed Police protection, and even longer before I realized that they enjoyed political protection. So, I became a reformer.

T.R.: And a damn good one.

STEFFENS: They're complaining about your tactics.

PARKHURST: It's hard to please criminals. You can never treat them in a manner that exactly suits their fancy.

T.R.: What brings you here?

PARKHURST: I've come on an unpleasant errand, Commissioner Roosevelt. I regret to inform you that there is still a certain reluctance to enforce the law despite the recent elections. Two saloons were open in violation of the Sunday closing laws last night. And, there are many bordellos that seem to be immune from all forms of attack. I was at one last night.

WATSON: Good Heavens–certainly you, a clergyman, didn't frequent a place like that?
PARKHURST: Certainly, I did, Dr. Watson. How else am I to prove that it was open?
WATSON: But surely, your position would not allow you to–
PARKHURST: Duty is duty, Dr. Watson.
HOLMES: Dr. Watson is thinking of–I quite see your point, Dr. Parkhurst. But an Anglican minister–
PARKHURST: I am an Anglican minister–
WATSON (*shuttering and sitting down*): Are you, sir?
PARKHURST: If I rely on the reports of others, they say I am only listening to unfounded gossip and rumor. So, I go myself. I make a very good witness.
HOLMES: Indeed, sir.
WATSON: But, how do you prove that–that–prostitution was actually going on, unless you–*Good God*!
PARKHURST: My methods are very thorough.
STEFFENS: You see, Dr. Watson, in America we pass laws in the confident hope that the Police will not enforce them. We are a very moral society. At that rate, we can afford to be.
PARKHURST: When I demanded the saloons and bawdy houses be closed, Mr. Holmes, the proprietors had the effrontery to say there was no need to change the law, because the law prohibited their activities anyway. When I demanded the law be enforced, they said it was impractical. Criminals always have an answer.
HOLMES: I have found that to be true myself.
PARKHURST: Now, we have replaced the Tammany politicians with a Reform administration. A new broom. We hope it will sweep cleaner than the old broom. Here is a list of the places that I can prove were open in violation of the laws. Good day, gentlemen.

(*Exit Parkhurst.*)

T.R. (*angrily*): Does he imply? Does he suggest? Doesn't he understand that we're on his side?
STEFFENS: He's only on God's side.
T.R.: Damned impractical Reformers. I'm doing all I can. But the fact is, it's hard to run against human nature.
STEFFENS: You see, Mr. Holmes, the honest working people of this city believe in observing the Sabbath. Hence, they passed a law that on Sunday, the saloons must close. But–
T.R.: But–as Sunday is their only day off, they want to have a drink or two.
HOLMES: Which they are unable to do if the law is enforced. I perfectly understand. It's hard being moral and having a thirst, too.
T.R.: I'm doing my best. I'm doing my best.

(*Enter Clubber Williams, a brutal looking man in the uniform of a Police Inspector.*)

WILLIAMS: Well–it's twelve o'clock, and I'm on time. So get it over with, shall we? (*seeing Steffens.*) You here, too? I should have expected it.
STEFFENS: I told you I'd stay here until you were forced out, Clubber.
WILLIAMS: Isn't it enough you plan to dismiss me? You want to humiliate me, too–you buck-toothed devil. Enjoy your triumph. (*grinding his teeth.*)
T.R.: I'll let that remark of yours pass–but only because you are under great stress, Inspector Williams. I summoned you here because I have to advise you that I

have reviewed your record with the Police Force and the accusations made against you by Inspector Schmittberger and others. If you like, we can postpone this until I can speak privately–
WILLIAMS: Let them stay, let them stay–
T.R.: Then, I must inform you, that I find the charges made against you credible and well-substantiated. Therefore, I have determined as President of the Police Board, that you must be dismissed from the force. The dismissal is effective immediately.
WILLIAMS (*tearing his medals off and grinding them under his heel*): After 25 years of service. All for bravery. And, they count for nothing.
T.R.: Your service record was taken into consideration. You will receive your pension. If you like, I will explain my reasons in detail.
WILLIAMS: That will be unnecessary. It's all because of that hypocritical Schmittberger. Good God, what fools we were to trust him–just because he looked like a cop. He–you'll live to regret this. Mark my words– Tammany Hall will come back to power in the next election. The people will soon be sick of all you goody-goodies.

(*Exit Williams in a rage.*)

HOLMES: Well, we seem destined to witness high drama today.
WATSON: Was his service record good?
STEFFENS: Oh, excellent. If you discount his corruption and brutality. He earned the name Clubber by being the nastiest man on the force with a nightstick. You would be amazed from a medical point-of-view, Dr. Watson, what can be done to a man with a nightstick.

T.R.: In many ways, he was a good officer. His brutality was directed against street toughs–men much worse than himself, vile street criminals, who, unfortunately, only understand brutality. In Williams, they met a man who spoke that language fluently.
WATSON: Still, you can't condone–
T.R.: I would have condoned it, much as I dislike it. But, I will not condone his corruption.
STEFFENS: To my mind, taking the money was the least of his faults. Taking money from saloonkeepers to stay open on Sundays is regarded as white graft–a harmless way of supplementing a police officer's low salary.
T.R.: He's rich.

(*Enter Parker, a dapper well-dressed little man. Roosevelt bristles immediately when Parker enters, like a horse in the presence of a snake. Parker is not in the least impressed by Roosevelt. The dislike is mutual, but somehow Parker always has the edge, and better control of his temper.*)

PARKER: I see you've done in poor Williams.
T.R.: I told you what my intentions were, Parker.
PARKER: You should have consulted the other members of the Police Board. There are four of us, remember?
T.R.: I announced what I was going to do.
PARKER: An announcement is not a consultation. Grant doesn't like it.

(*Parker exits, turning on his heel.*)

HOLMES: Who is he?

T.R.: That was Parker. He is also a member of the Police Board–and the leader of the opposition to my policies.
STEFFENS: They don't like each other.
HOLMES: An understatement.
T.R.: He thwarts me every way he can. And, by God, he is clever.
WATSON: Does he work for Tammany?
STEFFENS: Oh, no–he just can't stand being less than first. Grant–you know he's the son of our former President–almost always sides with Parker.
WATSON: Is this Grant an important person?
STEFFENS: He's a nonentity. Really, Parker is the great obstructionist. I told him privately what I thought of him. Enough to make most men ashamed, or ready to fight. All Parker said was: "Well, that has the virtue of being honest." I've never wanted to beat a man so much in all my life. He's insupportable.
T.R.: We can't stand each other. It's my character to say exactly what's on my mind. With Parker, I doubt if the left side of his brain would tell the right side of his brain what it was doing, even under a pledge of secrecy.
STEFFENS: He's devious and resourceful–and I can never figure out his motives.
T.R.: Bother Parker. Would you care to go out with me tonight, Mr. Holmes? I intend to see how the Police are performing their patrol duties.
HOLMES: That might prove interesting.
T.R.: Meet me at my hotel at 2 a.m. Steffens will be there, too.
WATSON: You can count on us.

BLACKOUT

Scene III

A dark street. On the left, a door to a tavern. By the tavern, an alley. On the right, a house with a red light in the window.

TAVERNKEEPER'S VOICE: Now, where is that damn cop? I suppose he's gone off to sleep in the alley again!

(*Enter T.R., Holmes, Watson and Steffens.*)

T.R. (*overhearing the Tavernkeeper*): I'll fetch him for you!

(*Suddenly, a woman screams from the alley. We see two men fighting. Roosevelt, Holmes and Watson rush in. Roosevelt grabs at a man with a knife, who slips free and retreats into the alley and disappears.*)

T.R.: The fellow is as slippery as an eel.
HOLMES: He runs fast for a club foot.

(*The second man reveals himself.*)

PARKHURST: Don't pursue him, Mr. Holmes, these alleys are veritable rookeries.
WATSON: Why, it's Dr. Parkhurst!
T.R.: What are you doing here?
PARKHURST: Visiting a brothel.
WATSON: By Jove!
PARKHURST: In the line of duty, you may rest assured. It is one of several that still remain open.

T.R.: Where is it? I'll shut it down myself.

PARKHURST: It's over there. But we can discuss that later. First, we must look to this lady. She was being attacked by that scoundrel when I intervened.

HOLMES: Are you all right, Madam? Dr. Watson can attend you, if you are hurt.

MRS. AVERY: I am perfectly all right. Dr. Parkhurst came to my rescue just in time, or I should be dead.

PARKHURST: Why–it's Mrs. Avery. Laura–what are you doing here? In such a neighborhood, and at such a time of night?

MRS. AVERY: I might ask you the same question, Dr. Parkhurst–but I am very glad to see you.

T.R.: This is no place for a lady. Why did you come here?

MRS. AVERY: I was following my husband.

PARKHURST: Mrs. Avery is a parishioner of mine. She's married to a man–a foreign gigolo by the name of Avery, and he has led her a very sad life. He is both insanely jealous, and totally unfaithful himself.

MRS. AVERY (*weeping*): I received a letter this morning advising me, in the friendliest way, that my husband would be visiting Dolly Well's brothel tonight. I thought, rather foolishly, to catch him in the act.

WATSON: Poor woman!

PARKHURST: Married to a brute!

T.R.: The hound deserves a good thrashing! But, it was hardly a wise decision.

MRS. AVERY: I shall be more prudent in the future.

HOLMES: Did you recognize your attacker?

MRS. AVERY: No, no. It was some ruffian who thought to snatch my purse or–or–

T.R.: The dog. If I catch him–

MRS. AVERY: It happened just after I dismissed my cab.
WATSON: Doubtless, he thought you–
MRS. AVERY: –That I was one of Dolly's girls! Oh, sir, I am mortally ashamed.
WATSON: You see where imprudence can lead a woman. In the future, you must consider the modesty of your sex.
HOLMES: Strange, that he should have attacked you immediately after you dismissed your cab–almost as if he were waiting–
T.R.: Probably some drunk who saw his chance.
STEFFENS: More likely, he was waiting for some man to be his victim, and thought a woman presented less likelihood of resistance.
HOLMES: Still–it's unusual. May I see the letter?
MRS. AVERY: What letter? Oh, that. I–uh–I no longer have it.
HOLMES: Indeed?
MRS. AVERY: I tore it up after I read it. I was very upset.
HOLMES: Of course. It was very lucky that Dr. Parkhurst was just coming out of Dolly's place.
PARKHURST: I am glad I was able to be of some assistance, Laura. But I am afraid he would have been too much for me, if it hadn't been for Mr. Roosevelt–and you, too, gentlemen. If you will allow me, Laura, I will accompany you home.
MRS. AVERY: I will be delighted. But my husband–
PARKHURST: I assure you, Laura, he wasn't there.
MRS. AVERY: Oh, why then, of course–
PARKHURST (*leading Mrs. Avery off*): I'll see you in the morning, gentlemen, and give you my full report.

(*Exit Mrs. Avery and Dr. Parkhurst.*)

T.R.: This is the strangest adventure I've ever had, gentlemen.
WATSON: I see he meant what he said about personally investigating these hell holes.
T.R.: He's absolutely fearless.
STEFFENS: Dr. Parkhurst will go anywhere vice is practiced. He knows himself to be incorruptible and therefore he does things a more prudent man wouldn't even consider doing. He cannot stand corruption. It makes him mad.
HOLMES: There's something more to this than–

(*Before Holmes can finish this thought, he is interrupted by loud singing from the brothel. Enter Clubber Williams and Parker, arm in arm, bellowing out "For He's a Jolly Good Fellow." Parker and Williams are happy and drunk. Roosevelt glares at them. When they see Roosevelt and company, the singing stops abruptly.*)

T.R.: This is hardly conduct becoming a member of the Police Board, Parker. As for you, Williams, I would say it is in character.
PARKER: I am simply trying to cheer up poor Clubber, on his retirement. A little innocent amusement.
STEFFENS: In a whorehouse?
PARKER: They have an excellent piano player, and the drinks are the best in town. *Honni soit qui mal y pense.*
T.R.: You make me sick, Parker, you don't even have the decency to be ashamed.
PARKER: Well, you can take your revenge, if you like. If you publish this, I shall have to resign.
T.R.: I have no intention of publishing this.

PARKER (*amused*): Really, why not?
T.R.: It's not my way.
PARKER: I warn you, I would do it if I were in your shoes.
T.R.: I have no intention of publishing it.
PARKER: Ah, but you will let your little reporter friend do it–a clever way to keep your conscience clean.
STEFFENS: I have no such qualms.
T.R.: Steffens, I'll strangle you, if you dare to publish this.
STEFFENS: But, Mr. President–
T.R.: I won't hear of it.
PARKER: You're a damn fool. But, thanks a lot. Shall we go, Clubber? Evenin' gents.
HOLMES: Before you go, Inspector Williams, I want to ask you some questions.
WILLIAMS: And who the 'ell may you be? I saw you this morning, but we weren't introduced.
T.R.: He's Sherlock Holmes–the English consulting detective.
WILLIAMS: And, what's he consulting about? How to fire me?
HOLMES: I've been asked to look into the Schmittberger matter.
WILLIAMS: Oh, the stoolie.
HOLMES: Are you aware there was an attempt on Schmittberger's life this afternoon?
WILLIAMS: Was there? I hope they got him.
HOLMES: No. Another man–a bystander was killed. You have a very clear motive for making such an attempt.
WILLIAMS: As does everyone else on the force that trusted that Judas. Why should I do it? I have my pension and my–uh–savings. No need.

PARKER: You don't have to answer any questions, Clubber.
WILLIAMS: What does it matter? I have an alibi.
T.R.: An alibi? You weren't even told when the attack occurred.
WILLIAMS: You think it's a secret? Everybody on the force knows about it. It occurred at two o'clock in front of O'Banion's Saloon. Well, at that time I was consulting with Commissioner Parker and Commissioner Grant about my possible retirement. So forget that.
HOLMES: Do you have any idea who might have done it?
WILLIAMS: Let me see. If I were investigating this case, I'd say the Police Commissioner himself had a very good motive.
T.R.: What? How dare you?
WILLIAMS: Schmittberger is an embarrassment to you–alive. You've kept on a man who is admittedly the bag man for Tammany. Dead–he's a hero and you can blame Tammany.
PARKER: Our dear President of the Board isn't smart enough to do that, Clubber. No, that theory won't work. Now, I might do that–but I'm not in Mr. Roosevelt's shoes so I have no motive.
T.R.: Don't waste time talking with these scoundrels, Mr. Holmes, they will not provide you with any useful information.
HOLMES: They may already have done so.
WATSON: Even in this uncivilized part of the world, it is preposterous to believe that a public official would kill a man simply to help his own political cause.
PARKER: It wouldn't be the first time. But, I think Steffens is behind it.

STEFFENS: What? You're insane.
PARKER: It would sell some more newspapers. Evenin' gents.

(*Exit Parker and Williams, laughing, into the alley. They begin to sing.*)

T.R.: Of all the effrontery.
STEFFENS: Let me print it, let me print it.
T.R.: No. Or I'm done with you.

(*Suddenly, the singing stops. Parker and Williams return.*)

T.R. (*not noticing Parker and Williams*): Well, gentlemen, shall we continue our rounds?
HOLMES: Lead on–Mr. Parker, what's wrong?
PARKER: There's a policeman in the alley–with his throat cut.
WILLIAMS: I know him, too. His name is O'Hara. His job is to act as a bouncer at Dolly's and the saloon next door. He does a few rounds. He's an old man and would never hurt a fly. They cut his throat from ear to ear. (*weeping, maudlin.*)
T.R.: Who would do such a thing?
HOLMES: I can't prove it. But, I will venture a guess. The ruffian who was waiting for Mrs. Avery.
T.R.: But, why?
HOLMES: Now, that is the mystery.

BLACKOUT

Scene IV

Roosevelt's office, the next morning. An exercise horse and several other types of equipment have been added to the furniture. There is a noise of hammering. Roosevelt is by himself, doing some exercises, when Holmes and Watson enter.

T.R.: Ah, there you are, Holmes.
HOLMES: Good morning, Mr. President.
T.R.: Excuse the disorder, I'm having a gymnasium installed in the next room, but the workmen haven't quite finished yet.
HOLMES (*as T.R. continues from one gyration to another*): Quite impressive.
T.R.: Would you like to wrestle?
HOLMES: Wrestle?
T.R.: We can have a tumble right now, if you like. I have some mats.
HOLMES: No thank you, I abhor all forms of exercise.
T.R.: You don't say! But, I understood you are familiar with the oriental martial arts.
HOLMES: I have a slight acquaintance with jiu-jitsu and several other martial arts, but only for professional reasons. I much prefer to exercise my mind instead of my body.
T.R.: Is that so? (*somewhat incredulous.*) Well, as you please. Perhaps you, Dr. Watson?
WATSON: Thank you, no, Mr. Roosevelt.
T.R.: Well, perhaps you box?
WATSON: No, no. I mean, yes I do, but, no, I'd rather not.

T.R.: Well, I shall just have to hire a sparring partner, I suppose.

WATSON (*aside to Holmes*): Maybe if we could get him to lie down, the fever for exercise would pass.

T.R.: Another murder was committed last night. Not far from here, either. A very strange case.

HOLMES: Indeed. What happened?

T.R.: Someone murdered an organ grinder here in Mulberry Street. Brutal and senseless, and it's raising a lot of fuss in Little Italy. The old man was very popular.

HOLMES: What was the motive?

T.R.: Robbery.

HOLMES: I would hardy think an organ grinder would have much money.

T.R.: They don't. At least, this one didn't. They stole his organ and his monkey.

WATSON: But, that's the strangest thing I ever heard of. Is no one safe in this barbaric country?

(*Enter Dr. Parkhurst.*)

PARKHURST: Ah, Mr. Roosevelt, Mr. Holmes. I am very glad to see you here.

T.R.: About that brothel–

PARKHURST: Never mind that.

T.R.: Why, but I've–

PARKHURST: Mrs. Avery has disappeared. I saw her home last night. This morning, I called on the way here to see if she had recovered from her fright. Her maid said that directly after I brought her home, she changed clothes and went out again. She hasn't returned.

HOLMES: You had better tell us all you know about Mrs. Avery.

PARKHURST: Really, I know very little. She joined my parish several months ago and became a member of the choir. She is very wealthy and married to a jealous Italian Prince or something.

T.R.: Married to an Italian. But, she uses an English name.

PARKHURST: He changed his name because it's difficult to pronounce. Anyway, he used to make scenes and accused his wife of having affairs with practically anyone she met. It was quite distressing. A madman, without a doubt.

HOLMES: Go on.

PARKHURST: Naturally, she separated from him.

HOLMES: And?

PARKHURST: She became friends with Sidney Gray.

T.R.: Sidney Gray?

PARKHURST: Yes. Why–

T.R.: But, that is the name of the man who was killed in the attack on Schmittberger!

HOLMES: Now, I think we can begin to see to the bottom of this mystery.

T.R.: Do you? Well, I confess, I can't.

HOLMES: And, how did Mrs. Avery's husband react to her friendship with Sidney Gray?

PARKHURST: He caused a row–or I should say several rows. Very distasteful.

T.R.: And, I believe he even accused you of some involvement with his wife, did he not?

PARKHURST (*flabbergasted*): How did you know that? Yes, yes, he did.

HOLMES: Tell me about Sidney Gray.

PARKHURST: He's a very well-to-do man. His family is socially quite prominent, but in a very quiet way. He

took a great interest in the Reform Movement. It is a shame about his death–
HOLMES: Sidney Gray was deliberately murdered.
T.R.: What? But, the bullet was intended for Schmittberger–
HOLMES: Gray was the target of the attack, not Schmittberger.
T.R.: But, the threatening letters to Schmittberger?
HOLMES: A ruse to divert suspicion from the person with a motive to attack Sidney Gray.
WATSON: But, who would want to attack Sidney Gray?
HOLMES: Why, Mrs. Avery's husband–who else?
T.R.: I see, I see. A love triangle. Jealous Italian husband. She may have been having an affair with Sidney Gray–
PARKHURST: I refuse to believe that. Sidney Gray was a man of high moral character–and rather naïve.
HOLMES: So much the worse for him. He probably refused to be blackmailed.
PARKHURST: Blackmailed?
HOLMES: Yes, of course. Don't you see that this wealthy lady with a jealous foreign husband is a kind of vaudeville routine? Mrs. Avery and her husband have used this many times before, I have no doubt.
PARKHURST: If this is true–
HOLMES: You've met her husband?
PARKHURST: Yes. Several times.
HOLMES: He's a clubfoot, is he not?
PARKHURST: That's true, that's true! But, how–
HOLMES: How do I know? Because this pair are famous. He goes by the name Ricolletti. They've been active for some time on the continent. The woman poses as a wealthy American heiress who is estranged from her violent Italian husband. She joins a fashionable

congregation. She's Catholic, Jewish, Protestant, by turns. A whole Ecumenical conference. After a short time, she allows herself to be compromised by some wealthy church member–frequently the minister.

PARKHURST: What an escape I have had!

HOLMES: The jealous husband appears and catches the guilty lovers in the act. He threatens murder and exposure. This unsettles everyone. Finally, the woman proposes to give the worthless Italian some money to get rid of him. He's venal and he agrees. Now, she proposes to pay him from her own money. But, her money is all tied up in spendthrift trusts. Could the lover advance the money himself? She will pay him back.

T.R.: And, of course, that's the last one sees of either the lady or her husband.

WATSON: How diabolical.

PARKHURST: The woman must be a viper. But, I can hardly believe that Laura–

HOLMES: Believe me, Dr. Parkhurst, you've never met a woman in all your excursions into the cribs of New York who is her equal in vice and depravity.

T.R.: But, why was Gray killed?

HOLMES: Gray is a wealthy man. I think we may assume that Mrs. Avery and Ricolletti had a falling out.

T.R.: And–

HOLMES: Mrs. Avery decided to marry Sidney Gray, and to cut Ricolletti out. She may even have fallen in love.

PARKHURST: But, why has she disappeared?

HOLMES: To avoid her husband. Ricolletti has already given signs that he doesn't like her little trick.

T.R.: And, last night–the ruffian–

HOLMES: Exactly. The ruffian was a clubfoot!

T.R.: Then, it was Ricolletti.

PARKHURST: But, if she was trying to escape him, why would she follow him?
HOLMES: He was following her, not she him.
PARKHURST: Why would she seek refuge in a brothel?
HOLMES: Well, according to the information I have about Ricolletti's wife, that was where she began her career.
PARKHURST: Infamous! I trusted her. Excuse me, gentlemen, I am ill.

(*Dr. Parkhurst exits.*)

T.R.: I'll get every available policeman on the force looking for her.
HOLMES: Do so–before she is killed as well. Ricolletti is both cunning and ruthless.
WATSON: I hate to say this, Holmes, but could Parkhurst be involved? It was very singular his being in that part of town with Mrs. Avery last night.
HOLMES: The thought has crossed my mind.

(*Enter Schmittberger.*)

SCHMITTBERGER: Excuse me for interrupting Mr. Roosevelt, but there's been the strangest murder not two blocks from here.
T.R.: Out with it, man!
SCHMITTBERGER: A woman living in one of the Italian tenements has just been murdered by an organ grinder. She came to the window to listen to his music, and he stabbed her with a stiletto.
WATSON: And, last night, an organ grinder was killed–
T.R.: Did you catch the madman?
SCHMITTBERGER: No, sir. He escaped.

HOLMES: I'll wager, Mr. Roosevelt, that the dead woman is Laura Avery, and the organ itself belonged to the man killed last night.

WATSON: But, what would Laura Avery be doing in a tenement?

HOLMES: She probably thought it was safe to hide there. She speaks Italian.

T.R.: But, her husband's Italian–

HOLMES: I'm not so sure of that. Well, we'd better go see.

BLACKOUT

Scene V

A dark foggy street somewhere near the river. Several tenement houses.

(*Enter Holmes and Watson.*)

HOLMES: Come, Watson. I think we have tracked Ricolletti to his lair. Wait till I reconnoiter.

(*Holmes steps stealthily forward, then encounters a figure. A fierce struggle ensues.*)

WATSON (*lighting a lamp*): Commissioner Roosevelt!
T.R.: Sherlock Holmes! Is it you, Holmes? Well, I'm damned if I didn't take you for an Italian. What are you doing here?
HOLMES: I might ask you the same question.
T.R.: I received a tip that a man resembling the supposed organ grinder was seen hereabouts. When I saw you loitering, I thought–
HOLMES: No apologies. I have tracked Ricolletti here.
T.R.: Then, we have him.
HOLMES: I believe he is in this house.
T.R.: I have no warrant.
HOLMES: You Americans always have so many procedural difficulties. Watson and I will break in. You can say you observed us and followed us to apprehend us in the act.
T.R.: Bully!
HOLMES: Eh?

T.R.: Bully! It's an expression. It means splendid. By the way, you wrestle well for a man who abhors exercise.
HOLMES: Thank you, very much. You do quite well, too. Shall we begin?
T.R.: After you, gentlemen.

                                            BLACKOUT

Scene VI

Holmes and Watson fling open the door. Moriarty is seated at a large handsomely appointed desk. The room itself is luxuriously furnished.

HOLMES: Moriarty!
MORIARTY: None other! Do close the door, Holmes, there's a draft. Good to see you again, Dr. Watson.
WATSON: I am not aware that you and I have ever met, Professor Moriarty.
MORIARTY: It does not surprise me, Dr. Watson, that you are unaware of it. But, we have met, several times, in fact.
HOLMES: I am very fortunate. I knew you were in New York. Through tracing Ricolletti, I have happily killed two birds with one stone. Where is Ricolletti?
MORIARTY: He's gone where you will never find him. He's under *my* protection now.
HOLMES: Your protection! You will soon be in jail, too.
MORIARTY: On what charge?
HOLMES: There are several charges pending against you in England.
MORIARTY: Are there? I wired my solicitor this morning. None are pending.
HOLMES: What abut the Linden affair?
MORIARTY: During your absence, and mine, from England, the witnesses met with an unfortunate accident. Stung to death by a flight of killer bees. (*laughing*) You have no proofs against me anymore, Mr. Holmes.
HOLMES: You fiend!

MORIARTY: I knew you would follow me from England, my dear Sherlock. And, with you out of the way, I had this feeling that your case would somehow collapse.

(*Enter Roosevelt.*)

T.R.: Hands up. I am the Police. I saw a break-in occur here. You too, Mr. Ricolletti. (*brandishing a gun.*)
MORIARTY: Ah, Commissioner Roosevelt, I presume? Professor Moriarty.
T.R.: Moriarty. Shall I arrest him, Holmes?
HOLMES: Arrest him for aiding and abetting the escape of Ricolletti. Misprision of a felony.
MORIARTY: I have not aided Ricolletti in escaping. He came here and left here of his own accord. There are several witnesses to that, who can be produced, if necessary.
T.R.: If you are hiding a felon, I warn you—
MORIARTY: I am not hiding him—and I gave him no money. I merely offered him some advice. Besides, he was under no charges when he entered here. His name has never been mentioned in the Press. If I am arrested, I shall be released within hours—and I will sue you for false arrest. My attorneys advise me that I cannot be charged.
HOLMES: Is he correct, Mr. Roosevelt?
T.R.: I am afraid so, Mr. Holmes.
HOLMES: Damn—what a fool I've been.
MORIARTY: I assure you, I made it my business to inquire, Mr. Holmes. In fact, I remained here merely from a longing to see you again, after such a long time—and to advise you that I have taken an interest in this

matter. If you wish to charge me, I am at your disposal. My attorney is in the next room. Mr. Williams–

(*Enter Clubber Williams.*)

WILLIAMS: At your service, Professor Moriarty.
T.R.: What!
WILLIAMS: As a retired Police Officer, I have opened my private practice.
T.R.: You're not licensed.
WILLIAMS: Yes, I am. I studied for the bar at nights, and passed a year ago.
HOLMES: You win this round, Professor Moriarty. There will be others.
MORIARTY: Of course there will. I promise you that. But, rest assured, you would never have found me, if I had not decided to appear before you. It may surprise you to know that until yesterday, I was lodged within two doors of you.
HOLMES: I will track you down, I will track you down!
MORIARTY: I am above your petty persecutions, Mr. Sherlock Holmes. You may seek me wherever you like.
HOLMES: The duel will continue.
WILLIAMS: If you please, Professor, there's a point I would like to discuss with you privately.
MORIARTY: You will excuse us, Mr. Holmes.
WILLIAMS: The Professor is my first client, you see, and a most distinguished one, so you see, I'm a little nervous, and I want to be very correct.

(*Williams opens a door for the Professor.*)

HOLMES: The duel will continue.

MORIARTY: Certainly, Mr. Holmes, certainly. Till next we meet.

(*Professor Moriarty and Williams exit.*)

HOLMES: Moriarty has made a fool of me, Watson.
T.R.: Clubber Williams is laughing at me, Mr. Holmes.
WATSON (*facing the audience as the light darkens*): Ricolletti was never found. Holmes eventually surmised that Moriarty had done away with him in order to possess himself of the blackmail hoard Ricolletti and his abominable wife had amassed. That seemed to be the likeliest explanation, for neither Holmes nor Roosevelt were able to find the least trace of him.
HOLMES (*facing the audience*): Watson, Watson, what a fool I've been. There was no Ricolletti.
WATSON: No Ricolletti?
T.R.: But, what do you mean?
HOLMES: Ricolletti was Moriarty in disguise. A disguise so perfect that no one, not even I, recognized him. He has slipped the noose again.
WATSON (*facing the audience*): Moriarty vanished as he said he would–but Holmes was soon on this track again. This time the trail led to Peking and the Boxer Rebellion. As for Roosevelt, he went on to become Secretary of the Navy, and then to pursue a distinguished career that led to triumph after triumph. But to Sherlock Holmes, he will always be the Mulberry Street Irregular.

CURTAIN

The Man Who Fell From Heaven

Characters

Sherlock Holmes, a consulting detective
Dr. Watson, his roommate and confidant
Jack Clinton, a painter
Dr. Gerald Manly
Evelyn Manly, his sister
Nellie Ashford, a widow
Inspector Murray of Scotland Yard
Dr. McKay, a forensic pathologist
Mrs. Norton

Scene I
A sick room in Dr. Manly's home

Jack Clinton lies asleep in bed. Dr. Watson is conferring with Dr. Gerald Manly.

WATSON: Well, he'll be all right, I think. Nervous shock, a frail disposition, but I think, Gerald, there is no danger.
GERALD: That's my opinion, too, Dr. Watson, but since Clinton is my future brother-in-law, I thought it behooved me to get a second opinion. We aren't colleagues for nothing.
WATSON: What an extraordinary occurrence, Gerald. I am not at all surprised at his reaction. I dare say I would have had a heart attack.
GERALD: What! After all your adventures with Sherlock Holmes? You must have the nerves of a mountain lion.
WATSON: Yes, but I've been prepared for my adventures beforehand. I've never had a dead body drop through a skylight in the middle of a horrendous thunder storm.
GERALD: Yes, a most hair-raising event–still–poor Clinton was not exactly a model of fortitude.
WATSON: You say he's an artist?
GERALD: Yes. Pretty good, if I am any judge. And he actually makes a living from it.

(*Enter Evelyn, a lovely young woman in her early twenties.*)

EVELYN: Ah, Gerald, dear. And Dr. Watson. How is he?

GERALD: Dr. Watson has confirmed my diagnosis–nervous shock, nothing more. In a month your fiancé will be fit as a fiddle.

EVELYN (*looking fondly at Clinton*): Thank you for coming, Dr. Watson.

WATSON: I could hardly do less, after all, Dr. Manly is an old friend.

EVELYN: I just don't see why a burglar would pick Gerald's studio to burglarize.

WATSON: There's no predicting what criminals will do.

EVELYN: Well, falling through the skylight served him perfectly right. But, good God, it nearly killed Jack.

WATSON: Well, rest is the best thing for him. Don't worry, he'll pull out of it.

GERALD: I think your opinion goes a long way to reassuring my sister. Evelyn doesn't believe me. I'm only her brother, doctor or not.

EVELYN: Oh, Gerald, you know I think you're the very best doctor there is.

GERALD: Anyway, Watson, let's leave the nurse to her patient.

WATSON: Frankly, with such a pretty nurse, I should contrive to remain sick, if I were Clinton.

GERALD (*ushering Watson out*): Come along, Dr. Watson. I'm interested in hearing some account of your friend Mr. Holmes.

WATSON: I haven't been to see Holmes lately–

(*Watson and Gerald exit. Evelyn goes about the room, opens the window, plumps the pillows for Clinton. Voice of newspaper hawker outside can be heard.*)

VOICE: Well-known resident of Finchley Road lost in Channel! Body not found! Read all about it! (*fading*) Well-known resident lost at sea–
JACK (*starting up*): What was that?
EVELYN (*alarmed*): Please keep calm, Jack dear.
JACK: "Body?" I'm sure I made out "body."
EVELYN: Lie down at once and be still, you bad boy.
JACK: Please tell me what's going on, Evelyn. Is it about the other night?
EVELYN: Heavens no! That's old hat by now. No–the latest sensation is that a man was washed overboard apparently–and it wasn't discovered until the boat reached Ostend.
JACK: Oh–who was it?
EVELYN: Robert Ashfield. Gerald knows him. Now, be still and try not to get excited. I've got the paper already.
JACK: I knew Ashfield, too.
EVELYN: How?
JACK: I painted his wife's portrait.
EVELYN (*taking up a newspaper and reading*): "A cablegram from Ostend was received at Dover early this morning announcing that on arrival of the mail boat, one of the passengers was found to be missing. There can be little doubt that the missing man was Robert Ashfield, of Leadenhall, and Coombs Hall, Finchley Road, the owner of considerable tea plantations in Ceylon and widely known in the city." It's a very sad thing, isn't it?
JACK: Yes. I believe I did his wife's portrait a year or so ago. An extraordinary woman. A real beauty.

(*Dr. Manly returns.*)

GERALD: Ah–our patient is up.

EVELYN: The newsboys have been seriously disturbing poor Jack.
GERALD: Something astonishing has come to light.
EVELYN: What is it?
GERALD: The body that came through the skylight has been identified.
JACK: What? Who was it?
GERALD: That's the amazing thing.
EVELYN: What's amazing about it?
GERALD: The body has been identified as belonging to Robert Ashfield–who was washed off the Dover boat.
JACK: But, that can't be possible.
GERALD: Of course, it can't be possible. It's a case of mistaken identity, I'm sure.
JACK: What a strange coincidence.
GERALD: Jack will have to be present at the inquest– more's the pity. He's not so ill as to have an excuse for not appearing.
EVELYN: Gerald, I'm frightened.
GERALD: Don't be absurd. There's no danger.

(*There is a knock on the door. Gerald goes out and returns with Inspector Murray and Dr. McKay.*)

GERALD: I will permit you to question him, but try not to get him too excited.
MURRAY: Certainly, Dr. Manly, certainly.
GERALD (*to Clinton*): John, Inspector Murray and Dr. McKay would like to ask you a few questions. Are you up to it?
JACK: I'll do my best.
MURRAY: Good afternoon, ma'am.
EVELYN: Good afternoon.
GERALD: My sister Evelyn, and Mr. Clinton's fiancée.

MURRAY: Pleased to meet you, ma'am. Not to waste your time, sir, could we begin? You are a painter, I believe?
JACK: Yes, sir. An artist. Portrait painter, to be exact.
MURRAY: You're 30 years old?
JACK: Yes, sir.
MURRAY: And how long have you occupied the studio?
JACK: Oh, about two years.
McKAY: Can you describe it for us?
JACK: It's an old building set back from the road. I can't say how old. It's ideal for an artist. The models' retiring room is curtained off. The top light over it is in the center of the roof–about six feet by four, and divided into separate panels.
McKAY: Can the skylight be opened?
JACK: I believe it can, but I have never done so.
MURRAY: How far is it from the floor to the skylight?
JACK: About 25 feet, I believe. There are two doors to the studio. The main entry opens on a vestibule. The vestibule, in turn, opens into the body of the studio. There is an entry in the back which opens directly into the models' room.
MURRAY: Were both doors locked during your absence?
JACK: Certainly. I came in through the front door–and I had both the ordinary key and the latch key.
MURRAY: Can you say positively that duplicates of these keys have never existed?
JACK: I can't quite go that far. I've never seen a duplicate and never had any made.
MURRAY: The back door opens with the same keys?

JACK: No. The back door is opened with a separate key. The door is always locked from the inside. I never use it myself.
MURRAY: Where is that key now?
JACK: In the lock, I suppose.
MURRAY: Are you sure you did not take it away with you?
JACK: Possible, but I don't think so.
MURRAY: How long had you been absent?
JACK: I left town on Tuesday a week ago.
MURRAY: It was known to your friends that you would be absent for several months?
JACK: They knew I would be gone a considerable period of time, yes.
GERALD: I told Clinton that he needed a rest. He's over-strained. He was to spend the summer in France.
MURRAY: What caused your unexpected return?
JACK: I got a cable about some important business, so I came back. It was late–a terrible crossing because of the weather–and I went straight to bed.
MURRAY: Where do you sleep?
JACK: Directly off the vestibule. I didn't go into the rest of the studio.
MURRAY: Did you fall asleep?
JACK: Yes. About one o'clock in the morning, I heard this tremendous crash and shattering glass. I got up to see what damage had been done, and I found this body in debris under a lot of glass.
MURRAY: Did you know the man?
JACK: No–he certainly didn't look familiar. When I perceived that life was extinct, I must have fainted. Then I recovered and must have gone for the Police.
MURRAY: You say "must have gone." Do you mean to suggest somebody else may have gone?

JACK: No. It comes back to me that I did speak to a Policeman.
MURRAY (*in a kindly manner*): It would help if you were a little more definite. Try to recall the exact course of events.
JACK: I fear I cannot. I was very exhausted from traveling. I did not even know at the time that I had hurt myself–and I was quite surprised the next morning to find my hands and feet were so severely cut.
MURRAY: Were your feet unprotected?
JACK: I believe I had slippers on.
MURRAY (*pulling slippers from under his coat*): These?
JACK: Yes. The soles are cut through.
McKAY: How is it you are able to state with certainty you were roused at one in the morning?
JACK: I really had no idea at the time. I deduced it from what I learned since.
MURRAY: Please try to be more careful. That sort of thing confuses the issue.
JACK: I'm sorry. I'm just trying to do my best.
GERALD: Really, Inspector–you can hardly expect a person in his condition to answer with absolute precision.
MURRAY (*dryly*): Quite so, Dr. Manly. (*pause*) You have a man who acts as a caretaker?
JACK: Yes. His name is Elias.
MURRAY: What sort of company does he keep?
JACK: Really, I can't say. He is sober and reliable. He is a Methodist. I believe his intelligence is somewhat limited.
MURRAY (*sharply, probably a Methodist himself*): I see no necessary connection between your last two remarks.

(*Gerald guffaws and receives a savage look from the Inspector.*)

JACK: I did not intend to suggest any.
MURRAY (*not quite mollified*): Indeed! Well, if Elias had bad acquaintances, he might have communicated your absence to them, might he not?
JACK: I suppose it possible–but I don't think he has bad acquaintances.
MURRAY: Let me say, Mr. Clinton, that this case presents certain difficulties. The deceased was found lying across a chair. His head hung down and rested against the floor. You were brought back to the house by a constable. You had a coat, but no socks on. Your boots were not laced. The slippers were found in the bathroom–with fragments of glass, wet with blood. Your hands and feet were badly cut. As for the deceased, his clothes were sopping wet. His face and head badly cut. There was no name on his watch. He had 11 pounds and some silver in his pockets. He had several handkerchiefs marked with the monogram "A." The deceased also wore an overcoat, but the maker's name was not on it. The frock-coat had, however, the maker's name intact. As far as the room itself was concerned, it was undisturbed–except that the key to the back door was not in the lock or anywhere to be found. We were able to go to the coat-maker who thought the coat had been made for Mr. Robert Ashfield a few weeks before. He later identified the body as belonging to Robert Ashfield.
EVELYN (*exclaiming*): The man who disappeared from the Dover Channel Boat!
MURRAY: Precisely.
GERALD: It's a case of mistaken identity, that's all.

MURRAY: No. The body has been positively identified by several persons. It is hardly the most extraordinary aspect of the case. Dr. McKay, would you please give your report.
McKAY: Certainly. I arrived on the scene after being summoned by the Constable. After satisfying myself that life was extinct, I proceeded to examine the body. I was greatly puzzled as to the manner of death.
GERALD: Why?
McKAY: That water was running from his garments was not astounding considering the heavy rainfall. But the inexplicable part was that the deceased presented every indication of having met his death by drowning.

(*There is a solemn silence.*)

McKAY: The whole body was completely cold. The eyes closed, the pupils dilated. There was a severe scalp wound on the back of the head, but serious though it was, it was not enough to cause death. The death was fairly recent, but not recent enough to have been caused by the fall from the skylight. These findings were confirmed on autopsy. The lungs were spongy and distended and contained froth. Finally, the stomach was full of water.
GERALD: What kind of water?
McKAY: Salt water.

(*Another long silence.*)

GERALD: Was there no other way death could have occurred?
McKAY: No. He suffocated from drowning.
GERALD: What about the scalp wound?

McKAY: It was not caused by the fall. It was caused by a blunt instrument.
GERALD: Well, this certainly seems to be a case for Sherlock Holmes himself!
MURRAY: There's no need to be flippant, Dr. Manly.
GERALD: I am quite serious, Inspector Murray. In fact, my colleague, Dr. Watson, who is Holmes' close associate, was here to examine Clinton less than an hour ago.
MURRAY (*unenthused*): Indeed. You know Dr. Watson?
GERALD: Very well. And, as you know, he is Holmes' amanuensis.

(*Murray looks irritated, but before he can say anything, there is a knock at the door.*)

EVELYN: I'll see to it.

(*She goes out.*)

JACK: You say the body has been positively identified as belong to Robert Ashfield?
MURRAY: By his wife–by his brother, by his business associates.
JACK: But, as I understand it, he was on the Dover Channel Boat earlier that night.
MURRAY: He was seen there, too, by his wife and–

(*Reenter Evelyn.*)

EVELYN: Gerald, Mrs. Ashfield has come to consult you.
MURRAY (*surprised*): Mrs. Ashfield?

GERALD: I am the family physician, as chance would have it.
MURRAY: Would you ask her to step in? This may prove a fortunate coincidence.
GERALD: Certainly, if she is well enough.

(*Gerald exits and returns momentarily with Mrs. Ashfield and her companion, Mrs. Norton. Everyone rises except Clinton, who bows while remaining seated in the bed.*)

GERALD: Mrs. Ashfield came to consult me because she had been unable to sleep. This is Mrs. Norton, her companion.
MURRAY: Mrs. Ashfield, I wonder if it would be possible for you to answer a few questions at this time.
MRS. ASHFIELD: Certainly, Inspector Murray. I will do everything I can to help.
MURRAY: I realize it is rather soon for a second interview, but–
MRS. ASHFIELD: It's quite all right. I have a strong constitution.
MURRAY: In that case, please tell us again how your husband came to make this fateful journey.
MRS. ASHFIELD: My husband told me he had business in Ostend. He told me about it on Saturday. At first he thought of going alone, but on Tuesday, it was settled we would go together. He went to the City that morning. About three o'clock I got a telegram to pack his razor. I met my husband at the Cannon Street Station–he was very late and in a hurry. When we arrived at Dover, there was no fog, but the weather was foul, and I was nervous to go on. So I sent the baggage to the Lord Warden hotel. I went on board with my husband for a few

minutes. I actually stayed on the quay till the boat put out. Then I went to the hotel.

MURRAY: When did you first learn your husband was lost at sea?

MRS. ASHFIELD: The next morning–by cable.

MURRAY: Is it possible your husband went off the boat after you had gone to the hotel?

MRS. ASHFIELD: Not unless he was rowed ashore or the boat came back.

MURRAY: Was he a good sailor?

MRS. ASHFIELD: I believe he was. He never complained of being ill at sea.

MURRAY: Do you have any idea how much money he had about him?

MRS. ASHFIELD: I can't say. He was not likely to be short when taking such a trip.

MURRAY: Are you certain of your identification of the body?

MRS. ASHFIELD (*showing emotion for the first time, sobbing*): Absolutely.

MURRAY: There you have it. The boat pulled out at near midnight with Ashfield on board. Then sometime around one in the morning Mr. Ashfield comes crashing through Mr. Clinton's skylight. There was no train back to London after midnight and several witnesses place Ashfield on the boat.

GERALD: If we accept the conclusion to which we seem to be forced–then we must question our beliefs in the established order of the universe.

(*Silence. All stare at Gerald and no one speaks as the lights go slowly down.*)

BLACKOUT

Scene II
Jack Clinton's studio

Clinton is having tea with Mrs. Ashfield.

MRS. ASHFIELD: You artists are such romantic beings to us poor average people. It is quite thrilling to be allowed to enter your workshops.

JACK: I fear you will miss the thrill. Thanks to Evelyn the place is more like a drawing room than what I am used to. My cherished tradition of dirt and disorder have been disenthroned.

MRS. ASHFIELD: I almost feel as if I were usurping Evelyn's place. (*pouring tea.*) Pity she can't be here. She is so sweet that one really can't see enough of her. Too bad she had to be with those tiresome people this afternoon. Don't look so horrified, Mr. Clinton. Evelyn told me herself they were horrible.

JACK: Do I look horrified? I was doing my best to look sympathetic—on Evelyn's account, of course.

MRS. ASHFIELD: Of course, you look sympathetic. Please look sympathetic again—for me, this time.

JACK (*laughs*): Ha, ha.

MRS. ASHFIELD: I was expecting a wan smile—but you are so much in love that you cannot even spare that for another. Byron must have libeled men when he wrote: "Man's love is of man's life, a thing apart. The woman's whole existence."

JACK: He certainly stole it from the French—which makes him a double criminal.

MRS. ASHFIELD: I do not like coupling the word criminal with a name like Byron's. A genius can do no wrong.
JACK: Yes, much can be forgiven genius.
MRS. ASHFIELD: Any crime. Much, too, should be forgiven to people who are the reverse of geniuses.
JACK (*genially*): I am quite willing to forgive all such people.
MRS. ASHFIELD: Do you know that I have persuaded Mr. Sherlock Holmes to investigate the mystery?
JACK: Really?
MRS. ASHFIELD: He attended the inquest–in disguise, of course.
JACK: It strikes me Sherlock Holmes is a bit of a humbug.
MRS. ASHFIELD: I think so, too. But there's no denying his ability. He wants to see you.
JACK: Certainly. But I doubt I can tell him more than I told the Coroner.
MRS. ASHFIELD: I insisted he make an appointment. Otherwise, he might pop up in the middle of the floor. I shouldn't be surprised if he pretends he was hidden under your bed that terrible night.
JACK: It would be convenient if he had been. I'm afraid, however, that even Sherlock Holmes may be forced to declare himself beaten by this case.
MRS. ASHFIELD (*glumly*): The inquest was very thorough.
JACK: Still–the verdict was a little perplexing. "Found drowned." In the middle of London on dry land.
MRS. ASHFIELD: It was the only possible verdict. The only possible conclusion.
JACK (*wryly*): A miracle. Did I tell you that a minister wanted to preach a sermon in my studio?

MRS. ASHFIELD: What have you done with it?
JACK: I rented it to a Circus. They're selling tickets of admission. Doing quite a business.
MRS. ASHFIELD: How ridiculous.

(*A knock at the door.*)

MRS. ASHFIELD: That will be the celebrated Sherlock Holmes.
JACK (*going to the door*): I'll let him in. This should be interesting.

(*Enter Sherlock Holmes.*)

HOLMES: I know you very well by sight, Mr. Clinton– and I am very pleased to have this opportunity of making your acquaintance. What a great improvement this studio is upon your last.
JACK (*annoyed at Holmes' one-upmanship*): Did you pay sixpence, a shilling or a half-crown to see my old place?
HOLMES: I am not in the habit of making useless outlays–and so I took great care to pay my visit before the place passed into the hands of the showman. In fact, I was there the very morning after this–well, curious corpse made its inconsiderate descent upon you.
MRS. ASHFIELD: Would it be indiscreet to ask how you're getting along?
HOLMES: By no means. To be quite frank, I fancy I'm beginning to see daylight. There are one or two vital points in the theory that I've formed that are still wanting–and that's just the trouble. It's a devilish case.
JACK: So most people said.

HOLMES: Not in that sense. It's just my way of cursing. But I know I am on the right track. I've never known my instinct to mislead me.

JACK: I presume you consider I can be of assistance to you?

HOLMES: Obviously. Else, I should scarcely have the good fortune to be here now.

JACK (*ironic*): You are most kind.

HOLMES: You will understand that I cannot at this stage mention anything of the conclusions at which I have arrived. I merely wished to have a chat with you about your manservant.

JACK: About Elias? Well, I shouldn't be inclined to think any harm of him. He is rather a bore. He inflicts his little religious sermons on one and it is almost impossible to remain polite.

HOLMES: I suppose that is when he poses? You see I am not unacquainted with your doings. I know you use him as a model.

JACK: I shouldn't be surprised if you knew my thoughts even when I'm sleeping.

HOLMES: I don't mind being chaffed. But, I particularly want to know if you've noticed anything in his manner of late that has attracted your attention.

JACK: Well, he has struck me as cheerful–unusual for one of his religious beliefs. Also, he looked rather well fed.

HOLMES: In fact, as if he had been having more money to spend than before?

JACK: Possibly. But I have no idea where he gets it. The truth is, I generally ignore Elias.

HOLMES: I'll tell you. He has been regularly employed in the afternoons by Mr. Cyrus Ashfield.

MRS. ASHFIELD: My husband's twin brother.

HOLMES: Indeed. And it appears that Cyrus Ashfield, after grubbing along rather modestly for 20 years–has suddenly developed energy as great–as great, let us say, as that of his late twin brother.

JACK: But, didn't his brother leave him a good deal of money?

HOLMES: One third of the estate. One third to Mrs. Ashfield–and one third divided between the children of his first marriage.

JACK: Well–that explains it. Why shouldn't Elias be cheerful?

HOLMES: Yes. But why should Cyrus Ashfield hire Elias?

JACK: That is rather a coincidence.

HOLMES: I am of your opinion. Well, I have taken enough of your time, Mr. Clinton. Oh, by the way, I had the honor of calling on Dr. Manly last night. I made the acquaintance of his charming sister. What delightful people they are!

JACK: Sorry I couldn't be of more help.

HOLMES: On the contrary, my dear Mr. Clinton, this interview has been indispensable, indispensable.

(*Holmes bows and leaves.*)

MRS. ASHFIELD (*after Holmes leaves*): I think that man is a complete idiot!

BLACKOUT

Scene III
Jack Clinton's studio

Jack is working on a picture. He is evidently not satisfied with it. There is a quiet knock and Mrs. Ashfield slips in.

MRS. ASHFIELD: May I come in? Why, you look quite pleased–and I was really prepared to find you looking black at being disturbed. You must be much more angelic than I gave you credit for.
JACK: I wish it were in my power to live up to your conception of me.
MRS. ASHFIELD: What charming modesty. But, go on painting. I suppose you can work and listen at the same time.
JACK (*lightly*): I shall try.
MRS. ASHFIELD: What I've really come about is to ask you to dinner tonight. The guest of the evening is to be Mr. Sherlock Holmes. Dr. Manly has promised to come. Evelyn is enchanted, and I am to give you her message that you are to be enchanted, too.
JACK: Only because Evelyn says so.
MRS. ASHFIELD (*with mock chagrin*): Oh, dear–if I am to be so completely ignored as that, I shall feel merely as a woman just a little bit jealous.
JACK: It is really unkind of you, Mrs. Ashfield, to embarrass me with such a speech. Fortunately, I am convinced you do not in the least believe what you reproach me with.

MRS. ASHFIELD: What is the use of denial when you see through me so thoroughly. What penalty do you impose on me, Sir Judge?

(*Clinton stubbornly works at his painting.*)

MRS. ASHFIELD: What a terrible question I've put to you. I only just realize it. (*pause*) But, you will be wondering why this sudden reunion this evening.
JACK: You don't mean to say Mr. Holmes has–
MRS. ASHFIELD: He has not.
JACK: Then what has he done to deserve to be feted tonight?
MRS. ASHFIELD: It's for what he's going to do.
JACK: But isn't that rather imprudent flattery?
MRS. ASHFIELD: Oh, no. He's going to tell us his theories and explain his difficulties.
JACK: So. I misunderstood.
MRS. ASHFIELD: But enough of myself. Let me praise your picture for a change.
JACK: I had much rather you talk about yourself than praise my picture.
MRS. ASHFIELD: Is my praise worth so little?
JACK: Again, you pretend to mistake my meaning.
MRS. ASHFIELD: I plead guilty, Sir Judge.

(*Pause.*)

JACK: You have no definite plans?
MRS. ASHFIELD: I have not made them definitely yet. I think I had rather praise the picture after all.
JACK (*referring to the picture*): How do you think Evelyn has come out?

MRS. ASHFIELD: She is just kissable! I suppose you will be setting to work on the last figure now.
JACK: Immediately–that is imperative.
MRS. ASHFIELD: Of course, you have a model coming in. Is she as pretty as Evelyn?
JACK: I fear she is not. That is, the one I have in mind. In fact, the girl is impossible.
MRS. ASHFIELD: Oh!
JACK: I shall have to find someone else.
MRS. ASHFIELD: But won't that delay–?
JACK: Yes, but there's no alternative–unless–
MRS. ASHFIELD: Unless?
JACK (*getting it out with difficulty*): Unless you would sit for the figure.
MRS. ASHFIELD: I shall be delighted.
JACK: It will have to be nude.
MRS. ASHFIELD: I don't mind at all.
JACK: I–
MRS. ASHFIELD: Yes, Jack, dear–
JACK: I'm afraid Evelyn might mind–
MRS. ASHFIELD: Well, let's not tell her. It will be *entre nous*. I shall expect you then–before half past seven.
JACK (*defeated completely*): I shall be punctual.

(*Mrs. Ashfield leaves with an air of triumph. Jack slumps down with his head in his hands. The shadow of Sherlock Holmes appears by the window.*)

BLACKOUT

Scene IV
Mrs. Ashfield's drawing room,
after dinner that same night

Holmes, Mrs. Ashfield, Clinton, and Gerald and Evelyn Manly are present.

HOLMES: As I explained to Mr. Clinton, I took care to visit his studio before it had become a public recreation. But I had nothing there to help me. The only basis I had to work upon was the verbatim of the inquest. (*pulling a pamphlet from his pocket.*) My idea was to subject this report to a searching examination. Early in the proceedings, the Coroner, who was very able by the way, considered the examination of Mr. Clinton's servant Elias of some importance, but later abandoned that line of inquiry. Now it struck me that here was a track that might be followed with advantage–and so it has proved.
JACK: Nonsense! I beg your pardon. You must not take my exclamation literally. It was merely an expression of surprise.
HOLMES (*giving Clinton a cold look*): Quite a natural one, my dear, Mr. Clinton. I assure you, I take it as a compliment. But, to proceed. As you know, Mr. Clinton, Elias has been working for Mr. Cyrus Ashfield–and now seems to be flourishing rather suddenly.
GERALD: All this is interesting–but to what on Earth does it point?
HOLMES: In time, in time.
GERALD: I must confess that you make me feel quite thick-headed.

HOLMES: Perhaps you will soon have an opportunity of exercising your ingenuity and raising yourself in your own estimation, Dr. Manly. (*pause*) But, I have not yet finished with the inquest. Would you care to read the passage I have marked, Dr. Manly?

GERALD (*taking the manuscript*): Certainly.

HOLMES: This is the evidence of the porter on duty at the wharf gate.

GERALD (*reading*): The Coroner: You are perfectly sure you noticed who passed out?

Witness: Certainly, sir.

Coroner: You were not talking to anyone?

Witness: Only to–no, sir; nobody in particular.

Coroner: Then, you were talking to somebody?

Witness: Yes, sir.

Coroner: How, then, were you able to observe so carefully?

Witness: I was only talking just for a moment, sir.

JACK: What is all this about?

HOLMES: Have patience.

GERALD (*reading*): Coroner: How, then, were you able to observe so carefully?

Witness: I was only talking just for a moment, sir.

Coroner: To whom were you talking?

Witness: To Mr. Barham, sir.

Coroner: Who is Mr. Barham?

Witness: He's an aeronaut.

Coroner: An aeronaut?

Witness: Yes, sir.

Coroner: What was he doing on the wharf?

Witness: He only came for a chat.

HOLMES: You see the significance of this, I am sure?

(*Everyone looks helplessly on.*)

HOLMES: Undoubtedly, Barham was making a fool of the gate keeper. As for Elias, I do not think he was actively guilty. But I am sure he was in readiness to act– if called upon–and that he knew the crime was meditated.

MRS. ASHFIELD: Crime! Do you suggest there has been foul play?

HOLMES: I have no doubt whatever on that point.

GERALD: All this is indeed astonishing. Now, if you can explain the miracle away, I shall hold my head high once more. I never was so humiliated in my life as when, by ridiculing the affair, I gave Evelyn an opportunity of crowing over me–which she did most unmercifully.

HOLMES: I fear I have not yet succeeded so completely as that–but I have got quite far enough to hold you out the hope of crowing over your sister in your turn. I am sure Miss Manly will not be too peeved with me for helping her brother.

EVELYN: I shall admire you tremendously.

HOLMES: I must tell you further facts. One startling piece of news was that Cyrus Ashfield, the twin brother of the deceased was at Dover on the same eventful Wednesday evening in the company of the aeronaut Peter Barham.

MRS. ASHFIELD: That is certainly a coincidence.

HOLMES: This Barham makes balloon descents and takes passengers for a fee. Now finally, I learned that a full-sized balloon was observed, three days later by the Danish boat *Horsa* from Copenhagen, drifting across the North Sea. A long rope was suspended from the car.

GERALD: Incredible!

HOLMES: All these facts have been established.

MRS. ASHFIELD: I am beginning to be frightened of you.

HOLMES: My dear Mrs. Ashfield, I assure you, I'm a perfectly harmless sort of mortal.

JACK: And you believe that somehow Ashfield was murdered–drowned at Dover, put in the balloon which apparently blew out of control and discharged poor Ashfield on my skylight? Then the balloon blew out to sea–

GERALD: It's totally improbable.

HOLMES: I have not yet succeeded in constructing a perfect theory. The facts are suggestive–but how exactly it could have been done, I am driven to admit, I don't yet know.

JACK: How long would it take for the balloon to get to London?

HOLMES: According to the most expert calculations I have been able to obtain, about one hour.

GERALD: But, how the dickens did they get Ashfield off the boat? He was last seen on the boat.

HOLMES: That is the damnable part of it.

EVELYN: Maybe this Barham fellow followed the boat in his balloon. Then he could have caught Mr. Ashfield with a grappling hook.

GERALD: Bravo, Evelyn! But, how would that have caused Ashfield to drown?

EVELYN (*seeing the dilemma*): Oh, dear!

HOLMES: I think your suggestion is impossible.

GERALD: I'm certain there's a simple explanation we're all overlooking.

MRS. ASHFIELD: It certainly is tantalizing to feel oneself so evidently on track, yet to be utterly foiled in this way.

JACK: Is there enough evidence to arrest the brother?

HOLMES: Cyrus Ashfield? No–
GERALD: But the circumstances are so suspicious–
JACK: I have it. Splendid!
EVELYN: Jack has it!
JACK: Why, it's really simple. Cyrus Ashfield must have somehow lured Ashfield off the boat. Once off the boat, he could easily have been drowned, then set adrift in the balloon.
HOLMES: That is an extremely brilliant explanation–the only trouble is, Cyrus Ashfield spent the night in a hotel where he was seen by many persons before the time the Dover boat left with his brother.
JACK: Well, maybe Barham did the actual murder.
HOLMES: Possibly. But we cannot prove any motive.
JACK: Money–from Cyrus Ashfield.
HOLMES: Good–but so far, I am unable to prove that. There's one other possibility.
MRS. ASHFIELD: What is that?
HOLMES: That Robert Ashfield is still alive.
JACK: Then, who came through my skylight?
HOLMES: Why, Cyrus Ashfield.
MRS. ASHFIELD: Are you saying my husband murdered his own brother, and is now taking his place?
HOLMES: It's a decided possibility. The problem is motive.
JACK: Why murder your brother so you can pretend to be him and inherit a third of what you already have?
HOLMES: There seems to be no motive at all for Robert Ashfield to have wanted to kill his brother. It seems unlikely that the richer brother would be content to change places with Cyrus since Robert occupied a magnificent position, and his brother Cyrus was little better than a petty shopkeeper.
GERALD: There's no motive.

MRS. ASHFIELD: Much as I respect your judgment, I don't believe a word of it.
HOLMES: The trouble is, neither would a jury. There's a piece of the puzzle that's missing. When we find it, everything will fall in place.
JACK: But, will we find it?
HOLMES: Who knows? I will do my best.

                                                BLACKOUT

Scene V
Clinton's studio

Jack is talking to Mrs. Ashfield who has just arrived.

MRS. ASHFIELD: Dear friend, I hope you do not mind my coming to you so soon again. I always feel happy in this studio. By the way, I had a letter from dear Evelyn. I am sorry her brother's still so depressed.
JACK: Yes, he should never have gone with Sherlock Holmes to Dover. He needs a rest–and now he's bothering his brains about this seemingly insoluble mystery. Once Gerald's mind starts puzzling him about something–
MRS. ASHFIELD: Yes, Gerald has a real intellect. Mr. Holmes has written me, too, about his theory.
JACK: And does he still hold by it?
MRS. ASHFIELD: He believes eventually he will be able to determine how it was done.
JACK: Does he still think your brother-in-law is your husband?
MRS. ASHFIELD: That's ridiculous. Cyrus, he certainly is–and not Robert. I do hope it isn't true about Cyrus murdering Robert. I cannot believe he would do it.
JACK: You told me a while ago you had some idea of traveling. Have you decided?
MRS. ASHFIELD: I am in the same nebulous condition as before. And, as I have no real need to make up my mind–I don't. How's the painting coming along?
JACK: Better–since I started using you as a model.
MRS. ASHFIELD: Do you know, I like being your model.

JACK: Do you?

MRS. ASHFIELD: I believed all those silly romantic ideas of artists–getting involved, shall we say, with their models. Very romantic.

JACK (*strangled*): Do you?

MRS. ASHFIELD (*removing her clothes*): But you always behave with perfect decorum. What a surprise for the public who think something quite scandalous is going on? (*suddenly, to Jack, who has turned away, after looking at her hungrily.*) Why do we keep up this meaningless fencing, this half hinting at our inner lives? I want to see me growing under your hand. Why should Evelyn be here day after day–and not I–who love you! Why? And you feel the same. Conscience has made cowards of us both.

JACK: It's true. I've been a coward. It's a wonder we both haven't gone mad. Evelyn has felt the change in me. I can never make her happy now.

MRS. ASHFIELD: Evelyn is too good. I love her myself. Even if you never see any more of me, you mustn't marry her unless you love her. She's too good for that.

JACK: Yes, she is far too good for that. But why do you talk of my seeing you no more? I must see you. I know Evelyn. Her nature is not like ours. She can bear pain with resignation.

MRS. ASHFIELD: But, will she heal?

JACK: This love of ours is a divine gift. Shall we scorn it? Shall we regret it? Love is here with us now. Happiness is a precious thing, Nellie. Have we a right to cast it from us? Can we make such a sacrifice?

MRS. ASHFIELD: Sacrifice! Sacrifice is for the strong. Let us both frankly admit we are not strong. (*kissing him.*) Is it not delicious to be weak?

JACK: I have never loved anyone before. This–this alone is the real thing.
MRS. ASHFIELD: I am glad my husband died, dear. Because it brought me you.
JACK: I have a confession to make.
MRS. ASHFIELD: What is it?
JACK: I'm glad he's dead, too. Did you love your husband?
MRS. ASHFIELD: No. He was kind and good–and very fond of me. If you were very fond of me, I should kill myself. Five years of happiness–that's all I want of life.

(*Jack and Mrs. Ashfield embrace passionately. The shadow of Sherlock Holmes and then another figure appear briefly at the window as darkness falls.*)

BLACKOUT

Scene VI
Clinton's studio,
late at night

Clinton is pacing up and down in the studio. Gerald Manly comes in.

GERALD: Hello, Jack.
JACK: Oh, Gerald–your startled me.
GERALD: Sorry, old man.
JACK: Where's Evelyn?
GERALD: She's not feeling well. You look as if you were expecting someone.
JACK: As a matter of fact, yes. I was expecting Nellie.
GERALD: She won't be able to make it.
JACK: Is she sick?
GERALD: She's dead.
JACK: That's impossible!
GERALD: I was called in, but it was too late.
JACK: But how? I just saw her this morning–
GERALD: Suicide.
JACK: No–no. Not Nellie.
GERALD: I thought I'd better tell you myself. I know you've become involved with her.
JACK: I'm sorry, Gerald. I know you must feel I've betrayed Evelyn.
GERALD: Oh, never mind on that score. Do you have a drink? I could use one– and so, I think, could you.
JACK: Yes, yes, of course–over there.
GERALD: I'll get them.

(*Gerald goes to a cabinet and returns with brandy and two glasses.*)

GERALD (*pouring Jack a drink*): Here, now drink.

(*Jack drinks.*)

GERALD: That's a good fellow.
JACK (*quietly, more composed*): How did it happen?
GERALD: She took poison.
JACK: But, why, why? We were planning–
GERALD: She became despondent about her husband.
JACK: About her husband? But she loved me. I–I– That's crazy.
GERALD: No, Jack. She realized that her part in the murder could no longer be concealed.
JACK: Her part? What are you talking about?
GERALD: We–Nellie and I, planned his murder.
JACK: You!
GERALD (*laughing*): It was so simple, and it has given rise to such ridiculous nonsense.
JACK: You murdered Robert Ashfield?
GERALD: Jack, have you never suspected I was Nellie's lover? I rather pride myself it would have taken a shrewder man to suspect it. But, then I was never a hypocrite. All I did was keep it secret.
JACK (*in shock*): You were Nellie's lover?
GERALD: We became friends–dear friends–after I became the family physician about two years ago. She cared nothing for her husband. She absorbed all my philosophy–she grew to fear neither God nor the Devil. I alone made her life livable. I did all in my power to dazzle her–yet, she wouldn't admit she loved me. Of course, she yielded her body to me willingly enough.

JACK (*his head in his hands*): She never told me! Never!
GERALD: The fact is, Nellie was not always truthful. She worked me up to it–killing her dolt of a husband, I mean. She couldn't stand being tied to a man of so bloodless a disposition. She hated him. He was driving her mad with his boring kindness. At last an insidious thought came to both of us. At first we hardly dared speak of it. But if you want ideas to master you, resist their first approaches. The idea grew and grew. Then one day, she said, "Rid me of him." Rid her of him: I was quite ready.
JACK (*unbelieving*): You murdered him!
GERALD: Murder is a vulgar word. Don't be enslaved by tradition, Jack. You must look at reality. Nellie is a remarkable woman. Would the world be the worse off for the loss of a nonentity who differed in no way from thousands of others. His place could easily be filled.
JACK: I think you must be mad.
GERALD: Not unless it is madness to want to live with the woman you love. Anyway, we waited our chance. Immediately after you left London, our chance came. Robert Ashfield announced his intention of going to Dover. So you remember how I came to your studio before you left for France?
JACK: Certainly. To say goodbye.
GERALD: And to pocket the key to the back door to your studio. You see, I had decided where I would do it.
JACK: But Ashfield was drowned at sea.
GERALD: We'll come to that. That is the best joke of all. You see, Ashfield never intended to take Nellie with him. But he did ask her to purchase the ticket. She bought two tickets.
JACK: Why two tickets?

GERALD: Two tickets. Then she told everybody she was going to Dover with her husband. Nobody would doubt that.
JACK: Yes–but still–
GERALD: Ashfield, of course, never left London at all.
JACK: But how–?
GERALD: I met him on his way to the station, and insisted that he come with me to your studio.
JACK: To my studio? But, how were you able to get him to break a business engagement so easily?
GERALD: I showed him a love letter Nellie had written to you.
JACK: But she didn't write me any letters at that time. We hardly knew each other.
GERALD: But how was poor Ashfield to know that? I told him Nellie was your lover and that you were planning a tryst that very night in your old studio. I insisted we go there to surprise you both. The poor man was thunderstruck–docile as a lamb.
JACK: But how did you explain how you had got the letter?
GERALD: I said Evelyn had found it. After all, she was your betrothed.
JACK: Good God.
GERALD: And the writing was certainly genuine. So he came along. And when I got him there, I killed him.
JACK: But he drowned.
GERALD: My intent was to stun him and let him bleed to death. I thought he would be dead two months before you returned.
JACK: It was pure luck that I returned.
GERALD: Yes. I could hardly foresee that New York would make such a large offer for your work that you would have to return. Anyway, to get back to it. I seized

him as soon as I got in the house, and we struggled for some time. As it happened, we ended up in the bathroom. For some reason, there was water in the tub.
JACK: Elias was always forgetting to pull the plug.
GERALD: He begged me not to do it. But I remembered Nellie, and how happy we were to be–and I hardened my heart.
JACK: But the Coroner said he drowned in sea water!
GERALD: Yes, that amazed me too at first. That was the biggest farce of all. Then, I understood it. You will remember that when you persistently refused to leave England, I recommended as the next best thing that you take a hot bath with artificial sea salt added.
JACK: But Ashfield was seen on the boat!
GERALD: I accompanied Nellie to Dover. It was simple enough to answer to Ashfield's name–and then slip off the boat.
JACK: And Cyrus Ashfield–and Barham the aeronaut?
GERALD: Pure coincidence. We made our plans without consulting poor Cyrus, and had no intent to involve him. It took Sherlock Holmes to do that. Mr. Holmes, you see, has made a mystery where none existed.

(*Holmes and Watson step out of the shadows.*)

HOLMES: The only mystery, Dr. Manly, was how to get you to confess–because you had, more by accident than design, created the almost perfect crime.
GERALD: How did you guess?
HOLMES: Well, I examined the deceased's correspondence, with his wife's permission. I took the liberty of examining Mrs. Ashfield's correspondence as well, without telling her.

GERALD: And you found?
HOLMES: Several love letters to her including one from you.
GERALD: Ah!
HOLMES: From that point on, naturally, I knew what had happened, but proving it was decidedly difficult if one of you did not confess.
GERALD: Well–it seems I underestimated you, Mr. Holmes. My apologies.
WATSON: I should never have believed it, Dr. Manly, if I had not heard it from your own lips.
GERALD: Sorry I'm such a disappointment to you, Dr. Watson.
HOLMES: It only remains to add the denouement. After all your efforts to secure Mrs. Ashfield for yourself, she became enamoured of Mr. Clinton.
GERALD: Yes–it seems I committed the perfect crime only to benefit my rival and ruin my sister's happiness. And so, I told Nellie I was going to confess.
JACK: And Nellie committed suicide.
GERALD (*bitterly*): I only meant to bring her to her senses! I knew she was posing nude for you–and I knew to what end she would bring it.
HOLMES: It must have been a great disappointment for you, Dr. Manly.
GERALD: I didn't think she would do anything so foolish. Nellie was a noble creature–I tell you, Jack, she was good through and through. She told me she loved you and she begged me to release her from her promises to me. If she concealed the past from you, it was only because she wished to begin a new page of existence.
WATSON: Did you ever suffer from remorse?
GERALD: So far as the deed itself was concerned– never. Let the mob talk of murder, and let them glorify

men like Napoleon who kill by the thousands. I destroyed but one. However, the gods are even with me—if you must put a moral on it. The murder turned out to be utterly useless. The only thing I regret is my intense satisfaction at the time. I was free, I was happy, I was in love. Put not your faith in the heart of a woman, Jack! How could I foresee you would rob me of my Nellie?

JACK: I never intended to do it.

GERALD: Poor old fellow, you don't imagine how you have made me suffer—but I never bore you any ill will for it. I must tell you Evelyn has never suspected anything at all. You can go back to her. She merely felt a little disquiet. Evelyn is a good girl. Sometimes it is best not to be too clever. Cherish her and be happy.

HOLMES: I am afraid, Dr. Manly, that you will have to accompany us to Scotland Yard.

GERALD: Oh, no. I've a precaution against that. I wanted Jack to know. But, I prefer not to hang. (*biting poison.*) You see, I came well equipped.

(*Dr. Manly collapses; Watson runs to him.*)

WATSON: Cyanide!

GERALD: Goodbye, dear fellow. I die happy knowing I shall be resolved into raw dust. As for my cynicism, which you have always refused to take seriously—be assured that I am in earnest about it. (*dies.*)

WATSON: He's dead, Holmes.

JACK: How will I tell Evelyn?

HOLMES: Ah, Mr. Clinton, that is a mystery I am glad I am not obliged to solve.

CURTAIN

Clash of the Vampires

(*Sherlock Holmes and Dracula*)

Characters

Sherlock Holmes, a consulting detective
Count Dracula, a Vampire
Inspector Lestrade of Scotland Yard
Queen Victoria
Wallace, a Palace Official
A Police Sergeant

The story takes place in London in 1889.

Scene I

A London Street in a poor section of the city. A foggy night. The street is empty. A dim light is cast by a gas lamp.

AT RISE, the street is empty. Then, there is a movement in the shadows. But we cannot make out what it is. A woman is heard laughing. A door shuts. More female drunken laughter.

After a while, we make out a figure emerging from the fog. It's Sherlock Holmes, deerstalker and all. He's on the track of someone and looks very preoccupied. From the opposite direction, Count Dracula emerges from the fog. He's very elegant in his cape and top hat. He carries a cane which he twirls. The two men bump into each other.

DRACULA: Ah, pardon me.
HOLMES: My, fault. I was preoccupied.
DRACULA: My condition exactly.
HOLMES (*recognizing Dracula*): Ah, Count Dracula, I believe.
DRACULA: Why, it's Sherlock Holmes!
HOLMES: In London again, Count?
DRACULA: Yes. But only for a short visit. The season has begun, and I'm expecting to take in a few events. I've grown accustomed to English ways, you see.
HOLMES: Too accustomed. I must say, you look very elegant and fit.(*The Count bows.*) Too fit.
DRACULA: I dine well.

HOLMES: I should rather you weren't here, Count. Is Transylvania too small for you?
DRACULA: After London, I should think so.
HOLMES: I shall do my best to make your stay here as unpleasant and as fruitless as possible.
DRACULA: Ah, bah! I defy you. But I am delighted to meet you again.
HOLMES: Indeed!
DRACULA: In fact, I was thinking of employing you.
HOLMES (*outraged*): Employing me? You must have lost your wits, Count.
DRACULA: Actually, I'm at my wits' end, Mr. Holmes. You remember our last encounter? [1]
HOLMES: Could I forget it?
DRACULA: Then, you remember that scoundrelly disgrace of a vampire, Lord Ruthven?
HOLMES: Certainly. I thought you had dealt with him.
DRACULA: As did I. But the insulting little eel managed to escape from the confinement I held him in.
HOLMES: How was he able to do that?
DRACULA: By a rascally trick, you may be sure. He corrupted one of my most trusted servants. What a disgrace he is to our vampire race.
HOLMES: He rather fancies himself an ornament to it.
DRACULA: He's in London! I'm here to get him back.
HOLMES: In London, why, that–
DRACULA: That means that all sorts of abominations are possible. No one in England is safe, especially women, not even the Queen.
HOLMES: The Devil you say!
DRACULA: He is a Devil with the ladies.

---

[1] *The Adventure of the Beneficent Vampire* in *Lord Ruthven the Vampire*, Black Coat Press, 2004 (ISBN 1-932983-10-4).

(*A woman can be heard moaning low. Holmes and Dracula both look embarrassed.*)

DRACULA: I want you to help me find him.
HOLMES: What will you do with him if you do find him?
DRACULA: This time, I plan to impale him.
HOLMES: Why should I help you?
DRACULA: Because if I catch him, there will be one less vampire in the world, whereas if you do not, knowing Ruthven, there will be many more, and–
HOLMES: Say no more, I will help you. But on one condition.
DRACULA: State it.
HOLMES: That you remove Lord Ruthven and yourself from England immediately.
DRACULA: Never to return?
HOLMES Never to return.
DRACULA: You drive a hard bargain, Mr. Holmes. England has its attractions. Especially, the ladies, and fashion, too, I–

(*At this moment, a bloodcurdling woman's scream pierces the night.*)

DRACULA: What was that?
HOLMES: I don't know. Can you tell where it came from?
DRACULA: I smell blood. In that direction. (*pointing.*)

(*Another scream. Then, silence.*)

BLACKOUT

Scene II

Inspector Lestrade's office in Scotland Yard. Everything is in perfect order. Not one paper is unfiled. Lestrade is sitting at his desk going through a file.

Holmes knocks. Lestrade looks up and gestures for the Detective to come in.

LESTRADE: You took your time getting here.
HOLMES: I came as soon as I got your message.
LESTRADE: All right, all right. I need to know why you showed up at the scene of the horrible murder last night in Whitechapel.
HOLMES: I was in the neighborhood and I heard the screaming.
LESTRADE: What time did you hear the poor woman?
HOLMES: Almost exactly 2:15 a.m.
LESTRADE: Why were you in the neighborhood?
HOLMES: I was retained by an estranged husband to discover if his wife was having a rendezvous.
LESTRADE: In Whitechapel? I didn't know you took clients like that, Mr. Holmes. A bit of a come down for you, the great consulting detective.
HOLMES (*grudgingly*): Yes, but the client offered a large sum, and even I must pay my bills.
LESTRADE: Doubtless. Did you see anything?
HOLMES: By the time I arrived, there was a crowd and the Police had the scene secured.
LESTRADE: You had a foreign bloke with you, I believe.
HOLMES: Yes.

LESTRADE: Your client?

HOLMES: No–an acquaintance.

LESTRADE: Did you see anybody prowl around, acting suspicious–anything?

HOLMES: Nothing of use, I'm afraid. What exactly happened?

LESTRADE: A poor woman was ripped apart.

HOLMES: Another Ripper murder?

LESTRADE: Very much like the ones we had before.

HOLMES: There was nothing in this morning's papers.

LESTRADE: Because we got there in time. Fortunately, it was late and there were no reporters around. We don't need to start another panic.

HOLMES: Whatever I can do, Lestrade–

LESTRADE: Cooperative, for once, eh? Well, you can start by telling me the name of your acquaintance. I shall want to question him.

HOLMES: His name is Count Dracula, Vlad Dracula.

LESTRADE (*nearly jumping out of his seat at the name*): Dracula! His bloodstained calling card was found clutched in the woman's hand!

HOLMES: But he couldn't be the murderer. We were several blocks away when we both heard the woman scream.

LESTRADE: That may be, but he's involved somehow. I must talk to him immediately.

HOLMES: He may be hard to find. And in any event, the Count never is to be found until after dark.

LESTRADE: I tell you, I want to see him immediately.

(*Holmes shrugs. A Police Sergeant enters clutching a newspaper.*)

SERGEANT: Sir, you'll want to read this.

LESTRADE: What? (*glancing at the paper the Sergeant hands him.*) *What?* But how can all this be? Who talked to the papers? Who?

SERGEANT: I am sure, Inspector Lestrade, that no one in the Department did.

LESTRADE: But someone must have. All the details of last night's murder are here. (*reads.*) Look at this, Holmes! You said there was nothing about it in the morning papers!

SERGEANT: It's an extra.

HOLMES (*reading*): "And the creature suspected of this savage crime is one Count Dracula, whose bloody calling card was found clutched in the hands of the hapless victim. This same Count Dracula is known to have resided in Transylvania where he is widely reputed to be a vampire–"

LESTRADE: A vampire–what rubbish.

HOLMES (*flatly*): He *is* a vampire.

LESTRADE: My eye! And you vouch for him?

HOLMES: Only that he was with me when the murder occurred.

                                                    BLACKOUT

Scene III

The Morgue. Holmes and Dracula are examining the body of the victim, one Mary Sheffield.

DRACULA: This is the work of Lord Ruthven, Mr. Holmes.
HOLMES: Were I not sure of the contrary, I'd think it was your handiwork.
DRACULA: Bah! I am not so crude. With me, feasting is an art.
HOLMES: Spare me your self-serving comments.
DRACULA: That little runt of Lord Ruthven is a brute, a real brute. He's bound to give vampirism a bad name.
HOLMES: Have you ever seen this woman before?
DRACULA: No, but she's a very beautiful girl. A real catch as they say. Do the Police know who she is?
HOLMES: No. The only identification she had was your calling card.
DRACULA: I don't use calling cards. The invention is too modern for my taste.
HOLMES: But why would she have it clutched in her hand?
DRACULA: It seems obvious to me, Mr. Holmes, that someone is trying to–I believe the expression you use is "frame me"–for this atrocity.
HOLMES: And you blame Lord Ruthven?
DRACULA: Who else? Who else would even suspect I am in England? I don't visit much.
HOLMES: But why should Ruthven try to blame you for his actions?

DRACULA: Lord Ruthven has a very twisted mind. He thinks like no one else, human or vampire. And that article in the paper? Clearly, he knows I am on his trail, and he would like to terrify the public, make them think I am responsible for his crimes, so as to give himself greater freedom of action.

HOLMES (*considering*): Despite myself, I find I am constrained to agree with you.

DRACULA: You must find him.

HOLMES: It's not easy. I'm a detective, not a vampire hunter, you know.

DRACULA: Think like a vampire.

HOLMES: That, I submit, is easier for you. Where do you think he is?

DRACULA: Lord Ruthven is very much unlike myself. I am of a retiring disposition, whereas he–

HOLMES: Is rather gregarious.

DRACULA: I am proud, but modest–Ruthven–

HOLMES: Is anything but modest.

DRACULA (*suddenly*): He'll be in society. He's a devil with the ladies. You'll find him dazzling young women somewhere. Oh, the brute. A ladies' man. A vampire. Really!

HOLMES (*looking at the body, again*): What level of society do you take this girl to be from, Count?

DRACULA: How should I know?

HOLMES: Observe. Her face?

DRACULA: Pretty delicate.

HOLMES: Well fed.

DRACULA: Apparently.

HOLMES: Her hands?

DRACULA: Clean and certainly not used to hard labor.

HOLMES: I think we may conclude that she's from the upper classes, or at least associates with them in some

genteel capacity. Perhaps a governess. Certainly not a working class girl from Whitechapel.
DRACULA: Has anyone been reported missing?
HOLMES: Strangely, no.

(*Enter Lestrade.*)

LESTRADE: Mr. Holmes. There's been an interesting development.
HOLMES: What is it?
LESTRADE: A man who claimed to be Count Dracula made an attempt on the Queen!
DRACULA: What? I am Count Dracula.
LESTRADE: You? But the fellow was a much younger man. He escaped, but dropped his calling card.
DRACULA (*with ferocious dignity*): Mr. Holmes, I demand that you find this impostor!

                                            BLACKOUT

Scene IV

A room in the Queen's Palace.

QUEEN: Mr. Holmes, my advisors tell me you are the only person who can get to the bottom of this.
HOLMES: Your Majesty flatters me.
QUEEN: It was the most horrible, horrible thing.
HOLMES: Please tell me exactly what happened.
QUEEN: I was alone in my room. I was writing a letter, and then I heard a slight noise, like–well, as if something had landed gently near the window. I looked up and there was this very handsome, slender young man. Fashionably dressed, but in the fashion of my youth. I gave a start. "Please, do not be disturbed by my unexpected visit, Your Majesty," he said. "Who are you and how did you get here? No one but my staff is allowed in my private apartments," I asked. "I beseech Your Majesty not to be alarmed," he replied. "I will be less alarmed if you answer my questions," I said. "I am Count Dracula and I've admired Your Majesty in silence for many years," he said. "Count Dracula? I've never heard of you. Where do you come from?" "From Transylvania. I came expressly to reveal my passion to you." "Your passion! What on Earth do you mean, Count?" "Why, my love, my undying love." "Surely you are mad. I'm an old woman." "Not only am I not mad, but I shall prove to you my undying affection." At that point, he tried to kiss me or–or bite me, I think. I screamed. "Ah, cruel, I only want to bite you on the neck," he said. At this point, Mr. Brown entered, responding to my cries for help. The self-styled Count ran off down the corridor and no one could catch him, and then he disappeared. He might still be here.

HOLMES: I doubt the so-called "Count" will reappear. He's already achieved his end.
QUEEN: But, other than frightening a woman of my age, what can it be?
HOLMES: Well, he clearly could have harmed you if that had been his intention.
QUEEN: Yes, Mr. Brown would not have been in time.
HOLMES: Then, I think we may rule out any intention to do more than scandalize you.
QUEEN: But why?
HOLMES: What better way than to insure that the British Government would be in full pursuit of Count Dracula, wherever he may be?
QUEEN: Why, in that case, this man was some impostor and not Count Dracula; someone wishing to harm Count Dracula?
HOLMES: Your Majesty's powers of deduction are very impressive.
QUEEN: Well, who was this imitation Count?
HOLMES: His name is Lord Ruthven. A vampire you will probably never have heard of.
QUEEN: Oh, but I should say I do know who he is. In my youth, I used to go to Scotland frequently, and Lord Ruthven was a very famous vampire in those days. He was said to look like Lord Byron. I never met him, but his outrages at Malvern were well-known. Of course, I did not believe in them. But why would he wish to injure this poor Count Dracula?
HOLMES: Well, Lord Ruthven is terrified of Count Dracula, who means to kill him.
QUEEN: Ah, I see. So if Count Dracula is blamed for frightening the Queen, then Lord Ruthven would have set all England after his nemesis.
HOLMES: Precisely.

QUEEN: And this Count Dracula is also a vampire, I suppose?
HOLMES: Yes.
QUEEN: And more powerful than Lord Ruthven?
HOLMES: Again, yes.
QUEEN: And this poor murdered girl that was found in Whitechapel last night, clutching the Count's calling card–she was also part of this scheme?
HOLMES: You know about the Whitechapel murder?
QUEEN: I am kept well informed of events likely to disturb the tranquility of my people.
HOLMES: Well, yes. It seems to be part of the same scheme, although–
QUEEN: Although?
HOLMES: I have a lingering doubt.

(*A palace official appears and knocks discreetly at the door.*)

QUEEN: What is it, Wallace?
WALLACE: There's an urgent message for Mr. Holmes from Inspector Lestrade. I was told that it was important enough that I should interrupt your meeting if it was still in progress.
QUEEN: Something very ominous has happened, I'm sure.
HOLMES (*after reading the message*): I beg Your Majesty's forgiveness. I must leave immediately.
QUEEN: Well, I'm going with you.
HOLMES: But–
QUEEN: I am not going to stay here in this palace with a vampire flitting about. Wallace, my cape.

BLACKOUT

Scene V

Holmes' Baker Street home. The Queen, wrapped in a black cloak, is seated in an armchair; Holmes is standing.

QUEEN: Do you think he'll come?
HOLMES: I have no doubt.
QUEEN: Brr! I'm going to meet a vampire.
HOLMES: He has exquisite manners. Nothing to be afraid of.
QUEEN: Oh, I'm not afraid. And anyway, I'm brave. What shall I do when he gets here?
HOLMES: Just sit there, Your Majesty. His business is with me.
QUEEN: Very well, I shall discreetly observe.

(*There's a brief knock at the door. The Queen and Holmes exchange a look. Holmes nods and goes to the door. The Queen pulls her wrap about her tighter.*)

HOLMES (*opening the door*): You are prompt, Count.

(*Enter Dracula.*)

DRACULA: You've found him?
HOLMES: Actually, he seems to have found me.
DRACULA: Where is he? Do you know?
HOLMES: I know.
DRACULA: Will you keep your word? I'm prepared to keep mine.
HOLMES: I will tell you all I know.

DRACULA (*with satisfaction*): Good. (*noticing the Queen.*) Ah, this must be the famous Mrs. Hudson. (*He bows before her, and before she can protest, kisses her hand.*)

QUEEN: Oh!

DRACULA: You cannot know how much I admire your famous lodger. My only regret is that I haven't met Doctor Watson.

HOLMES: Watson recently married.

DRACULA: Ah, my congratulations to him. (*abruptly*) Now, to business. Where is the scoundrel?

HOLMES: Unfortunately, he's made his escape.

DRACULA: You let him escape?

HOLMES: I was quite close to him, but he, evidently, was aware of it. He left me a letter.

DRACULA: A letter.

HOLMES: And enclosed one for you. (*He hands Dracula a small letter which Dracula grasps angrily.*)

DRACULA (*reading*): "My dear Vlad..." How dare the insolent puppy address me by my first name! (*continuing*) "By the time you receive this, I shall be far away, and you'll have to start your pursuit anew. But you might as well go back to Transylvania and prey on the local ignorant peasantry. You'll never catch me. You are dealing with an English Lord, not an uneducated Eastern European peasant. All you have succeeded in doing is to set the entire British Empire against you. I have informed Mr. Holmes that you were the butcher of that poor girl in Whitechapel two nights ago. You intended to make it look as if I were clumsily trying to frame you. First, you killed the girl. Then you provided yourself with a perfect alibi by getting one of your minions to employ Mr. Holmes on a pretended case of marital infidelity in the area, where you would meet him.

Then, it was simply a matter of having a woman scream. Diabolically clever. You easily convinced Mr. Holmes that you were innocent and that I was the murderer. Well, two can play at that game. I decided to visit the Queen and pretend to be you. Now the entire power of the British Empire is arrayed against you. Cheers. Lord Ruthven." You surely don't believe, Mr. Holmes–

HOLMES: Most surely, I do. It was very clever, Count. It only occurred to me later, that you could easily have killed the woman, and then deliberately met me under circumstances that did, I admit, convince me of your innocence. But one thing saved me. The maxim "Never trust a vampire."

DRACULA: Pshaw! You are being deceived, Mr. Holmes.

HOLMES: Possibly, but not by you.

QUEEN: You must leave my domains, Count Dracula. Immediately.

DRACULA: My dear Mrs. Hudson, I–

QUEEN (*letting her cloak fall off and rising*): I am not Mrs. Hudson.

DRACULA: Ah, pardon the mistake, Majesty.

QUEEN: You must go!

DRACULA: Very well. And Lord Ruthven? I shudder to think what will become of the British Empire with that scoundrel loose.

QUEEN: Leave that to me, sir. You've already committed one murder; there will be no more. Now go!

DRACULA (*bowing*): I obey.

(*Dracula vanishes as the lights suddenly go out.*)

HOLMES: He's gone.
QUEEN: Do you think he'll keep his word and leave?

HOLMES: Never trust a vampire.
QUEEN: I shan't. Now, I want you to find Lord Ruthven for me, Mr. Holmes. We can't have him flitting about, either.
HOLMES What shall I do with him, if I find him?
QUEEN: Oh, I don't know. He's such a cute little vampire. If only he were sincere. Don't say it, Mr. Holmes. I know. Never trust a vampire. But if you cannot trust a vampire as cute as that, who can you trust? You may escort me back to the palace, Mr. Holmes.
HOLMES: The ways of these vampires...

                                CURTAIN

The Silent Treatment

(*based on* The Tell-Tale Heart *by Edgar Allan Poe*)

The Man is led ON STAGE–which represents a small room–by Holmes and Watson. They gesture for him to sit down in a chair by a table. The room is completely devoid of furniture except for chairs and a table. The man sits down. Holmes sits across from him and looks at him. Watson remains standing.[2]

MAN: You think I'm mad don't you?

(*Neither of the two men say anything. They simply look at him. But they look at him in slightly different ways. Holmes looks stern; Watson, who is standing, smiles.*)

MAN: True–I'm nervous, very, very dreadfully nervous. (*he squirms in his chair.*) I am, it's true. (*he smiles.*) But (*wildly look at each in turn*) why will you say I'm mad?

(*Neither man responds verbally. Holmes remains seated and stares. Watson, standing, smiles slightly. The Man notices the smile and smiles back. Holmes, seated, frowns. Watson stops smiling.*)

MAN: The disease–I mean the nervous disorder–sharpened my senses–especially my sense of hearing.

---

[2] Alternatively, the men may be police or hospital orderlies. Or an all-woman cast may be substituted. The men may be dressed in period costumes or contemporary. Various styles of production are encouraged. But the Holmes and Watson characters must never utter a word.

(*He looks at them back and forth but, this time, both men remain expressionless, which makes the prisoner increasingly nervous.*)

MAN: My sense of hearing was very acute. I heard all the things in Heaven and on Earth. I also heard many things in Hell.

(*The interrogators look at each other skeptically.*)

MAN: How, then, am I mad? Listen, and observe how sanely, how calmly, I can tell you the whole story.

(*The men register interest. The whole story is what they want to hear.*)

MAN: The whole story. That's what you want, right? How it happened. How it started?

(*The men nod.*)

MAN (*with the look of a hunted animal*): It's impossible to say how the idea first got in my brain. But, once there, it haunted me day and night. Purpose, there was none. Passion, there was none.

(*The men smirk skeptically, then look at each other and nod.*)

MAN: I loved him. He was old, he'd never wronged me, never insulted me. I didn't want his money. It was his eye! Yes, it was his eye.

(*The men gesture impatiently.*)

MAN (*almost screaming*): One of his eyes resembled that of a vulture! A vulture, I tell you! Pale blue, with a film over it. Looked like a corpse. Whenever it fell on me, my blood ran cold. It made me shiver. (*he shivers just thinking about it.*) You don't believe me? You want to know which eye it was?

(*The men show no interest.*)

MAN: It was his left eye! So by degrees (*controlling himself*) I made up my mind to do something about it. But what could I do? I couldn't leave him–he was old, alone... (*passionately*) He needed me! He couldn't take care of himself without me. And who else would put up with him? Him, with that baleful eye? No one! No one. So, I had to do what I did.

(*He seems to collapse into silence. The men exchange a glance of skepticism, then look at him encouragingly. Holmes, seated, seems to insist he continue; Watson, still standing, allows a brief smile to cross his face that suggests it would be nice to continue.*)

MAN: Now this is the point. You fancy me mad...

(*They look as if they do.*)

MAN (*argumentatively*): But, you see, I'm not. Madmen know nothing–Ah, you should have seen me. You'd have been amazed how carefully, how wisely I proceeded–with what caution... (*insistently*) with what foresight–with what dissimulation, I went to work. Yes, I admit there was dissimulation. (*seeking sympathy*) But

I had to, for his sake. I loved him. I was never kinder to him than the whole week before I killed him.

(*The men begin to take notes.*)

MAN: I made his favorite food for him. I did everything I could think of to make his last days on Earth comfortable–not just comfortable, but delightful.

(*The two men look at him with something like the repulsion one feels in the presence of a snake. They momentarily forget their good cop, bad cop roles as interrogators, then resuming their parts with uneasy effort, they register interest.*)

MAN: Every night around midnight I turned the latch on his door and opened gently–oh, so gently. And then, I thrust my head in slowly, very slowly...

(*He first stands up, then falls to his knees. He mimes opening a door very carefully, very quietly, then slowly places his head in the room, inviting the Detectives to visualize as he does so. The two men watch with excitement. A long pause. The Man holds his head in the invisible doorway.*)

MAN: I didn't want to disturb his sleep. (*smiling at the men*) And I didn't. It took me an hour to place my whole head in the room. Would a madman have had so much self-control?

(*He beams at his interrogators. Holmes flashes his best smile of encouragement.*)

MAN: I took the flashlight–a small one, and turned it on, but I put my other hand over the lens so no light would wake him. Then, I opened my fingers so that just a single beam from the flashlight fell on his vulture eye. Then, I withdrew, cautiously, cautiously.

(*The men register disbelief.*)

MAN (*protesting*): I swear I did this for seven long nights. Every night, just at midnight. But the eye, that evil eye, was always closed. And so it was impossible to do the work. For it was not the old man who vexed me, but his evil eye. If only he'd kept it closed, I would still be going there, even tonight–shining my flashlight through my fingers.

(*The men look bored. They plainly want him to get to the point.*)

MAN: Every morning, I went boldly into his room asking him how he felt, inquiring how he'd passed the night. So you see, he'd have had to be a sly old man indeed to suspect that every night at midnight precisely, I was watching him as he slept.

(*The men look unimpressed.*)

MAN: The last night, the eighth night, I was more than usually cautious. Never before that night had I felt the extent of my powers, of my sagacity. I could scarcely conceal my feelings of triumph.

(*He stands up and opens the invisible door little by little.*)

MAN: It made me chuckle to think he was none the wiser. My feelings of triumph were difficult to contain. Perhaps, I actually did chuckle, because he sat up in bed as if he heard something. (*to the two men*) Now, you may think that I drew back, but no–the room was pitch black and I knew he couldn't see the opening of the door. I kept coming forward, steadily, steadily.

(*He opens the door very slowly.*)

MAN: I was just about to turn on the light when he sat bolt up right in bed crying out: "Who's there?"

(*The man looks at his two interrogators; they lean forward with tense interest.*)

MAN (*proud of his cunning*): I kept quite still and said nothing. (*pause*) For a whole hour, I did not move a muscle. He hadn't moved either. He was still sitting up in bed listening. But I was the stronger.

(*He sits down triumphantly. The men look as though they feel cheated but don't know what to do. Then he continues.*)

MAN (*matter-of-factly*): I was more patient, more in control than he. Presently, I heard a groan of mortal terror. I knew that sound. I've made it myself when all alone. (*he makes the sound of terror.*) I knew what the old man felt and pitied him. (*in a questioning tone*) Do you realize he'd been lying there awake since the first slight noise? (*he giggles*) I pitied him, although I chuckled at heart. He'd been saying to himself, "It's just the wind in the chimney, or possibly a mouse." Yes, he was trying to reassure himself. But all in vain. Because death was approaching him. He couldn't see me—or hear me—but he could feel my presence in the room.

(*He grasps one of Watson's hands and smiles; Watson shudders involuntarily. There is another pause. The two Detectives begin to act impatient.*)

MAN: I waited a long time, very patiently, before lighting my flashlight. You cannot imagine how careful I was, How I covered the lens—stealthily, stealthily, I let a little ray—oh, as fine as a spider's thread fall upon the vulture eye. (*wildly*) It was open—wide, wide open, and I grew furious as I gazed upon it. I saw it plainly—all a dull blue with a hideous veil over it that chilled the marrow in my bones.

(*The two men are increasingly absorbed despite themselves. They shiver involuntarily and forget momentarily to employ their wiles to urge him on—they rather wish he would stop.*)

MAN (*in a beseeching tone*): Have I not told you that what you mistake for madness is but over-acuteness of the senses? Now, I say, there came to my ears a low dull sound such as a watch makes when wrapped in cotton.

(*A dull thump-thump sound can bear faintly heard. The men look at each other as if they too, hear something.*)

MAN: I knew that sound well, too. It was the beating of the old man's heart. It increased my fury.

(*He stands up listening to the distant heartbeat.*)

MAN: But even yet, I kept still. I scarcely breathed. I remained motionless. I wanted to see how long I could look at the vulture's eye. Meantime, the hellish tattoo of the heart increased.

(*The thump-thump grows louder.*)

MAN: The old man's terror must have been extreme! It grew louder, I say louder every moment!

(*He goes to the men and clings to them in terror.*)

MAN: That beating–that endless, remorseless beating excited me to uncontrollable terror.

(*As he controls himself, the men, in relief, move away from him.*)

MAN (*calmly now*): Still, I stood still. But the beating grew louder! I thought I would lose my mind.

(*He begins to pace; the thump-thump gets perceptibly louder.*)

MAN (*wildly*): It was so loud! So loud! The neighbors would hear it if I didn't stop it. With a scream, I rushed toward the bed. He shrieked once, only once. (*suddenly perfectly calm*) Only once. I dragged him to the floor, and pulled the bed over him. Oh, that was a relief. I actually felt gay.

(*Holmes and Watson look at each other and nod. Then they look at the man again.*)

MAN (*in a worried tone*): But for many minutes the heart beat on with a muffled sound. This, however, did not vex me; it would not be heard through the wall. At length, it ceased. The old man was dead.

(*He bends down and places his ear against the body's heart.*)

MAN: I removed the bed and examined the corpse. Yes, he was stone dead. There was no pulsation. He was stone dead. At last, his eye would trouble me no more.

(*He stands up and speaks to the two men, calmly, with a relaxed air; the thumping has stopped.*)

MAN: If you still think me mad, you will think so no longer when I describe the wise precautions I took to conceal the body. There was a lot of work to do. First of all, I had to dismember the corpse. I cut off the head first, then the arms, then the legs.

(*As he removes each part, he demonstrates how he used a saw.*)

MAN: The legs were the hardest. I then took up the plank from the flooring in his room, and deposited all, carefully wrapped, between the scantlings. I then replaced the boards so cleverly, so cunningly that no human eye, not even his, could have detected anything wrong. There was nothing to wash out, no stain of any kind, no blood spot whatever. I had been too wary for that. A tub had caught all the blood. Ha! Ha!

(*The two men look at him puzzled.*)

MAN: Why didn't I just leave the body, place it back on the bed you ask? (*they nod*) No one would have suspected what happened. He was old, very old. The bed had left no mark. (*dejected*) It was a mistake, you're right. I should have thought of that. I cannot really say why I didn't.

(*A pause; the two men seem to urge him to continue.*)

MAN: When I had made an end of all those labors, it was four o'clock. Still dark as midnight. Suddenly, there was a knocking at the street door. I went down to open it with a light heart–for what had I to fear? There entered three men who introduced themselves with perfect suavity as officers of the Police. The neighbors had heard a shriek–and a complaint was lodged, and they had been deputed to search the premises. I could have demanded that they produce a warrant. But I was too clever for that. It might have aroused suspicion. Instead I smiled.

(*He smiles at the two men–who do not smile back.*)

MAN: For what had I to fear? I welcomed them. I explained the shriek was my own–in a dream. I told them the old man was in the country. I took them all over the house. I led them at length to his chamber. In the enthusiasm of my confidence, I brought in chairs and bade them rest, while I, myself, in the wild audacity of my perfect triumph, placed my own seat on the very planks beneath which I had so carefully placed the body.

(*He pulls up his chair closer to the man at the table. The two men look at him and laugh.*)

MAN: Yes, it was foolish of me. I realize that now. It was an act of hubris. But mark this! The officers were satisfied. My manner convinced them. (*he laughs*) They sat, while I answered cheerily. I was singularly at ease. They began to chat. How they bored me. Their idle chatter made my ears ring. My head started to ache, but still they chattered on, and the ringing in my ears increased. At length, I realized the noise was not in my ears.

(*A sound of a heart pumping begins to be just audible again, and increases until the end of the play at which point it is almost thunderous. As the beating becomes audible, the man stands up.*)

MAN (*troubled*): No doubt I now grew very pale. (*stops, and smiles at the two men, proud of his cleverness*) But I spoke more fluently, more suavely. (*suddenly dejected*) But the sound increased. (*the thump-thump intensifies*) (*wildly*) What could I do? It was a low dull sound, much like a watch makes when it is wrapped in cotton. (*he staggers*) I gasped for breath. I could hear it then. (*upset*) Just as I hear it now.

(*To Holmes and Watson, who don't hear it.*)

MAN: You hear it, don't you? Don't you?

(*The two men shrug negatively.*)

MAN: I began to talk louder and louder to drown out the noise of it! But the noise increased. (*the heartbeats increase*) Why couldn't they leave? I began to pace to and fro.

(*He begins pacing to and fro.*)

MAN: The men were looking at me strangely. The more they looked at me the more furious I became.

(*The two men stare steadily at him.*)

MAN: And the noise steadily increased. I had to drown that noise out. (*his voice gets louder and louder but the pounding heartbeat increases to over match him.*) O God! What could I do? I foamed. I raved. I swore!

(*He goes to the chair.*)

MAN: I took the chair and grated it on the boards but the noise rose over it.

(*He grates the chair to cover the noise; the thump-thump of the heartbeat increases.*)

MAN (*listening, then screaming*): It grew louder and louder!

(*The heartbeats begin to pound heavily. He has to struggle to make himself heard.*)

MAN: And still the men kept chatting, smiling. Was it possible they didn't hear it?

(*To Holmes and Watson who don't hear it.*)

MAN: You hear it, don't you? Don't you?

(*The two men shrug again.*)

MAN: They had to hear it. You have to hear it. They heard. They suspected. They knew. They were making a mockery of my horror. (*the thumping increases.*) Anything was better than this agony. Anything was more tolerable than this demon. I could bear those hypocritical smiles no longer.

(*The two men force themselves to smile at him.*)

MAN: I had to scream or die! And now–again–louder! Louder! Louder! Louder! (*as he screams, the thumping is at a crescendo.*) So I confessed– I confessed! (*the thump-thump is pulsating wildly.*) I confessed! Now make it stop! MAKE IT STOP!

(The thumping gets louder, louder. The Man hides his head in his hands, tries to plug his ears, begins beating his head against the wall. Holmes and Watson seem to talk to each other and write notes in their notebooks very calmly as the curtain falls. The heartbeats continue for some time thereafter.)

                                              CURTAIN

Notes:

The Man should always interact with the interrogators, never with the audience.

The two interrogators never hear the heartbeats. They are carefully taking notes of his behavior throughout.

**The Curious Circumstance
of the Maid's Mustache**

WATSON: I think this time I shall have bit of a surprise for you, Holmes.
HOLMES: Indeed, Watson, that will be a new experience. What is it?
WATSON: The Maid, Mrs. Jermyn.
HOLMES: Ah, yes, the autopsy.
WATSON: It was rather interesting.
HOLMES: The cause of death was accidental, Watson.
WATSON (*stunned*): We came to that conclusion, Holmes. But how did you know that?
HOLMES (*smugly*): I think I shall keep that to myself at present.
WATSON (*astounded*): Astounding! You were able to deduce that?
HOLMES: Do go on. You haven't surprised me quite yet.
WATSON: But that was not what was so surprising, Holmes.
HOLMES (*surprised*): Indeed? Something else proved surprising?
WATSON: Why, yes, rather.
HOLMES: What was it, Watson. That the body had been moved?
WATSON: No, although we arrived at that conclusion, too. You deduced that? You really are amazing, Holmes.
HOLMES: Or that the deceased had recently visited the sea?
WATSON: You noticed that, too, eh?
HOLMES: And that, I think exhausts your list of surprises does it not?
WATSON: Well, no, not quite.

HOLMES: Was it the curious circumstance of the two left shoes?
WATSON: No, not that.
HOLMES: Well, well, my dear fellow; this must certainly have been a shocker.
WATSON: It was. Frankly, it wasn't evident until we had removed the deceased's clothes.
HOLMES (*curious himself*): Well. What was it, dear fellow?
WATSON: The Maid, Mrs. Jermyn, was a man.
HOLMES: A man?
WATSON: A man!
HOLMES: This is rather a surprise, Watson.
WATSON: It was for me, too, I assure you.
HOLMES: It puts, as it were, a whole new complexion on the case.
WATSON: It does indeed, Holmes.
HOLMES: It rather causes me to question my powers of observation, Watson.
WATSON (*agreeably*): Yes, it does cause one to do that. (*Holmes glares at Watson.*) That is to say–
HOLMES: Well, well, this is surprising.
WATSON: I thought you'd find it so.
HOLMES: I detest surprises, Watson.
WATSON: I understand that, Holmes.
HOLMES: Surprises are disagreeable.
WATSON (*agreeably*): Indeed, Holmes, quite disagreeable.
HOLMES: They confuse one's thoughts.
WATSON: Often, I've noticed that myself.
HOLMES: It is entirely explicable why I did not notice this peculiarity, Watson.
WATSON: Quite so, Holmes.

HOLMES: There are many women who have mustaches and smoke cigars.
WATSON: Quite so, Holmes. It's the deplorable state of morality–
HOLMES: It could have happened to anyone, Watson.
WATSON: I quite agree, Holmes.
HOLMES: There was no reason to assume that just because Mrs. Jermyn had certain male features–
WATSON: Not the slightest in the world, Holmes.
HOLMES: It would have been rude to refer to it.
WATSON: Absolutely.
HOLMES: Un-English.
WATSON: But what do you suppose it means, Holmes?
HOLMES: It means, it means that Mrs. Jermyn was Mr. Jermyn, Watson.
WATSON: Yes, yes, quite so, Holmes. But what does it signify, Holmes?
HOLMES. That the deceased was curiously careless about gender, Watson.
WATSON: An Englishman should always be meticulous about gender, Holmes. I've always said so.
HOLMES: We don't want any of these continental hermaphrodites knocking about England!
WATSON: Hear! Hear! Not in Merry England.
HOLMES: If they're going to do that sort of thing, they should be sent to France!
WATSON: An Englishman for my money!
HOLMES: I'm with you there, Watson.
WATSON: None of that here in this sceptered isle.

CURTAIN

Printed in the United States
48609LVS00001B/20